NANCY WARREN

ᴬSPELLING MISTAKE

VAMPIRE BOOK CLUB
BOOK THREE

Ambleside Publishing

INTRODUCTION

Spell in haste, repent at leisure.

Middle-aged witch Quinn Callahan agrees to hold a book launch for the bestselling but recently dead author Bartholomew Branson. It's a small favor for the new vampire. Unfortunately, things get out of hand when the author arranges a huge launch party and someone dies.

Spells are going wrong, the book contains a dreadful mistake and the town of Ballydehag, Ireland, is once again in turmoil.

If you haven't met Rafe Crosyer yet, he's the gorgeous, sexy vampire in *The Vampire Knitting Club* series. You can get his origin story free when you join Nancy's no-spam newsletter at NancyWarrenAuthor.com.

Come join Nancy in her private Facebook group where we talk about books, knitting, pets and life.
www.facebook.com/groups/NancyWarrenKnitwits

ACKNOWLEDGMENTS

I was at a writing retreat in California when the Vampire Book Club series was born. Ny, Skully, Shelley, Linda, Jenny and Jackie, thank you so much for the brilliant ideas and the placemat plotting. I am so grateful for your support and generosity.

Linda Hall, you arrived one day in my inbox with your sharp eye and joy in language. You make my books so much better. Thank you, Linda!

Nancy Warren's Knitwits, where would I be without your wit and wisdom every day on Facebook? Thanks for your support, your memes, and good humor. I appreciate every one of you.

Thanks also to Judy, Jacqui, Wilfrieda, Cindy, Jenny and every reader who takes the time to review my books or encourage their friends to read them. Thank you all!

A SPELLING MISTAKE

CHAPTER 1

*V*ampires aren't the most excitable of creatures. At least not usually. However, when the vampire book club met that Tuesday night, I felt waves of anger and sadness coming from Bartholomew Branson.

Bartholomew was the most recent member of the club, having only been turned a few months earlier. A world-famous thriller writer, Bartholomew had taken part in a cruise where his fans had adored him so much that he ended up getting drunk and attempting to demonstrate a dangerous stunt from one of his books.

The result would have been a watery grave off the coast of Ireland except that one of his fans was undead and, unable to bear seeing her favorite author perish, turned him into a vampire. He was too well-known to appear in public in a big city and had somehow ended up here, in the small town of Ballydehag in County Cork, where a quaint bookshop called The Blarney Tome was run by a witch. That would be me.

I held the late-night book club specially for my undead

neighbors who lived in Devil's Keep, a castle on the edge of town overlooking the ocean. There were ten vampires at tonight's meeting. I'd tried to get them talking about the Iris Murdoch novel they'd chosen, but Bartholomew's misery was so overwhelming, it muted discussion.

"*A Killer in His Sights* is going to be published next month, without me," he moaned. "The seventeenth Bartholomew Branson bestseller, and I won't be part of it."

Bartholomew was not happy. He wasn't a literary giant, and his thrillers would probably not stand the test of time, but he'd loved the limelight and lifestyle of a celebrity. Now, that life was over and he was forced to remain out of sight and keep a very low profile. His final book was being released posthumously, which meant he'd be completely left out of celebrating his last best-seller.

"I love launch parties," he said, his mouth drooping with self-pity. "The champagne, the book sales, the long line of fans waiting for autographs."

"The fleeting nature of undeserved fame," Oscar Wilde put in. Oscar had proven that his literary genius was as immortal as he was, and he never wasted an opportunity to put Bartholomew in his place. Far, far down the hierarchy of literature.

"I had so many books I still planned to write. My career was really taking off," Bartholomew wailed.

"Ambition is the last refuge of the failure," Oscar said, picking a piece of lint from his purple velvet suit.

Bartholomew rose and turned to Oscar, his hands fisting. "Look here, you Irish windbag, my fans love me. All I want is one final launch party. Is that too much to ask?"

I felt so bad for him. I glanced at Lochlan Balfour, who was the acknowledged leader of the local vampires. I sensed he was sympathetic, but no one could give Bartholomew Branson what he'd lost.

I did have something I could offer, and now seemed a good time to reveal it. "I have a surprise for you," I told the wretched thriller writer. "I've ordered two dozen hardcover copies of your new novel. I'll feature them in the front window of the store, and we'll read your book as our next book club selection." Bartholomew was always nominating his own books for the club and was consistently rejected, so I knew he'd be thrilled if we discussed his novel in book club.

"Pass me my smelling salts," Oscar moaned. "I'm about to faint with horror."

But Bartholomew didn't even hear the latest insult. He rushed up to me, picked me up off my feet and swung me in a circle. "That's a great idea, Quinn," he said. "We'll have my final book launch right here." Then he put me down and stepped back. "Wait. I've got an even better idea. We'll do the real launch here."

"But, Bartholomew—"

"Don't worry, Quinn. I'll take care of everything. I can't believe I didn't think of it myself. I know exactly how to get the launch moved here. All you have to do is sign the letters I'll dictate, and I guarantee you'll have top publishing brass and hundreds of eager fans crowding into The Blarney Tome." He chuckled and rubbed his hands together. "Oh, don't look so shocked. I know I can't be at the party, but I can watch. That's almost as good as being there. Quinn, this event will put your little bookshop on the map."

How had a small favor to make Bartholomew feel better turned into this truly terrible plan?

I could only hope that he'd overestimated his fame and his ability to organize a book launch from beyond the grave.

If his enthusiasm for the project continued, how would I stop him?

CHAPTER 2

I let myself into The Blarney Tome, as I did most mornings, with Cerridwen, my black cat familiar, at my heels. It was a crisp September morning, and I had that back-to-school feeling I always got at this time of year, as though it was time to put away the flip-flops and beach reads and get serious.

I had my work—opening the till, turning on the lights, and readying the store for customers. Cerridwen had hers—sniffing up and down the aisles, making sure no stray mice had invaded the premises while she wasn't on duty. She was also a playful little thing, and when she decided we were vermin-free, she liked to get her morning exercise by leaping up onto the chairs, climbing to the top of bookshelves and sometimes knocking books down in the process. She kept me entertained when there were no customers around.

But this morning, something was different. I knew it the second I walked in. So did the cat. We looked at each other, witch to familiar. Something or someone was inside. And it wasn't a mouse.

In that nanosecond, I made a decision. Would I back out again and go for help, or would I investigate? I decided to investigate. No doubt the presence I felt in the shop was just the leftover energy of the people and vampires who'd been spending time here lately. I'd have to find some time to do a cleansing spell and get rid of the negative vibe.

I walked in deeper, and that sense of jangled energy grew stronger. Cerridwen didn't undertake her usual mouse-hunting expedition. She stayed right by my heels. She meowed once, in case I hadn't noticed that something was off.

I took a quick scan of the main floor of the bookshop, and nothing seemed out of the ordinary. The books stood quietly on their shelves. The cash register was on its counter. The community bulletin board held the usual announcements and ads put up by locals.

I stood silent for a moment, listening. I heard a noise from upstairs. Once again, Cerridwen and I stared at each other. As loud as though she'd used words, she said, "Be careful."

I wasn't the bravest woman in Ireland, but I did have some skills as a witch. If there was a burglar up there, I thought I could handle them. Not that there was much to steal. Still, I grabbed the only weapon I could find, a broom, and stealthily crept up the spiral staircase that led to the floor above. Cerridwen followed behind me. I heard a groan and a bang. There was definitely someone up there. Ready with both broom and spells, I made my stealthy way to the top of the stairs and peeked into the big room that housed my desk, extra book stock, and a nice seating area where we ran the vampire book club. One of these days I was going to start a book club for mortals, but I hadn't gotten around to it yet.

I immediately saw what had caused both the noises and

the jangled atmosphere and leaned my broom against the wall, letting out a sigh of relief.

"Bartholomew, what are you doing here?" I asked. Bartholomew Branson was the picture of a distraught writer. He was sitting at my desk, in front of my computer, his hands making a mess of his hairstyle. I think that noise I'd heard was him hammering his fist on the desk.

He looked up at me. "What's another word for fanatic? I can't keep using the same word over and over again. I'm losing my touch."

"Obsessive?" I tried.

He stopped clutching his hair and dropped his hands back to the keyboard. Paused to think about it. "Not bad."

He typed the word, and then I repeated, "Bartholomew, what are you doing here?"

He looked put out and petulant. "What does it look like I'm doing? I'm writing. And I'd really appreciate some privacy."

It was hard not to laugh. He was every inch the celebrity author. Sadly, his celebrity was bigger than his talent, and everybody seemed to know that but him. Certainly, the vampire book club did. Especially his archenemy, Oscar Wilde, who made mincemeat of him with his sarcastic wit whenever the two met. I wondered if that was really why Bartholomew was here. If he was writing, Oscar would torment him mercilessly.

However, as Bartholomew Branson never ceased to remind him, the one author was a lot more famous than the other. In a hundred years, I was certain that people would still be reading Oscar Wilde and nobody would remember Bartholomew Branson, but for now, when he was such a newly minted vampire, he outsold Oscar Wilde by about ten thousand to one, which gave him some bragging rights.

"And what are you writing?"

He looked up as though it was the hugest imposition that I should keep interrupting him. "What do you think I'm writing? Shakespearean sonnets? It's a novel, Quinn. This is the first draft of *The Price of Vengeance*. That's the working title, anyway. What do you think? I always used to talk things like title and plot over with my agent, Philip Hazeltine, and my editor, Giles Montague, but I can't do that anymore. You'll have to do."

I wasn't thrilled to be the stand-in for his agent or his editor. Not only would I not be getting fifteen percent of his royalties, but I had my own business to run. "It's a fine title, Bartholomew." Then I asked, as gently as I could, "Why are you writing another book?"

"It's what I do. I woke up this morning with a great idea for my next plot." He held up his hands and flexed his fingers. "I have to get it down while the inspiration's flowing from the muse."

How did I delicately put this? "Bartholomew, you can't write any more books. You're dead." Okay, that wasn't my best effort at delicacy.

Once more he looked at me as though I were a few books short of a stack. "I believe the word you're looking for is undead, and I've had a brilliant idea."

Oh dear. When Bartholomew Branson got an idea, it was usually less than brilliant. "What is it?"

He looked at me in triumph. "You, my dear Quinn, are going to discover an unpublished manuscript by

Bartholomew Branson. Imagine the publishing sensation when my book is published posthumously."

"You've already got a book being published posthumously. *A Killer in His Sights.* Remember?"

He waved a hand as though he were waving away a fly. "But this is a manuscript no one knew about. Obviously, because I haven't written it yet."

I had a really bad feeling that he'd come up with this idea when we agreed to do a launch for what should have been his final book. I couldn't even begin to tell him how terrible this idea was, and so I decided not even to try. I'd have to get the other vampires to help talk him down. Perhaps we could convince him between us.

I backed away and said, "I'll leave you to it, then."

"Wait. Before you go, can you think of another word for apocalypse?"

"No, Bartholomew, I can't."

He waved me away. "Never mind. Never mind. The muse has never deserted me yet. Carry on, Quinn. And try not to make too much noise downstairs."

Even though he wasn't watching, I rolled my eyes. "I'll do my best."

I headed for the stairs, but Cerridwen decided to stay upstairs with the writer. The last I saw of her, she was jumping on the sofa bed and curling up.

I went back downstairs and finished opening up the shop. It didn't take long.

Then I decided to redo my front window and showcase thriller authors. With his new book coming out, Bartholomew's novels would be front and center.

And knowing I'd have scorn heaped upon me by Oscar

Wilde, I decided that next month I'd focus on classics by Irish authors. I'd even let Oscar choose which works to display.

It was amazing to me that the ego of a writer lived on long after they were officially dead.

I think if Lucinda, the previous proprietor of this shop, had warned me that I'd have to balance a lot of delicate vampire egos along with a coven of temperamental witches, I might have taken my chances and stayed back in the States. Even if I was *witcha non grata*.

I was busily pulling together a selection of Bartholomew Branson novels, along with Lee Child, John Grisham, and Irish mystery authors Tana French and Benjamin Black, when I had my first customer of the day, Karen Tate.

Karen ran a shop just down from mine on Main Street called Granny's Drawers, where she sold antiques and consignment items. It was always fun to poke through her collection of everything from mismatched china to clothing, old jewelry, and pieces of furniture. She'd also become a friend and, although she didn't know it, it turned out we were distantly related through a terrifying and nasty witch, Biddy O'Donnell, who'd recently, most unfortunately, been released from the underground prison where she'd been held for the last few hundred years.

Karen had inherited the O'Donnell house and put a lot of time and money into updating and renovating the grand old home so she could open a bed and breakfast inn. I was excited for her but for one tiny problem. Biddy had once owned the property and seemed to think she still had every right to live there.

While my witch sisters would no doubt prefer to have Biddy back in her underground prison, I'd weirdly become involved in shielding her from what I considered a terrible fate. Biddy wasn't a very nice witch, but she was family. I didn't think I could rehabilitate her or anything, but now that she'd taken up residence in the O'Donnell house, I was hoping she'd stick to the kind of gentle poltergeist activities that would draw tourists to Karen's B&B.

Karen was dressed for work, her red hair tied back, wearing a blue and purple paisley blouse over black trousers and a costume jewelry necklace made of chunky plastic flowers. She didn't look like a woman in the mood to buy books. She was bubbling over with excitement, and not of the literary kind. Her brown eyes sparkled behind her trendy eyeglasses.

"Quinn, you won't believe it. I was able to get the mattresses delivered early. They're coming this afternoon. All the renovation work is finished, and all I was waiting for was the new mattresses. I could be opening my bed and breakfast for business within a week."

I was so pleased for her. "That's great that everything's running so smoothly."

"There's only one very strange thing. There seems to be something wrong with the electrics."

"Oh?"

She looked genuinely puzzled. "I've got televisions in all the bedrooms, obviously, plus a bigger one in the lounge room. And no matter what I do, if I leave the room and come back, the same program is playing."

"That's odd. What show is it?"

She might have thought it was an odd question, but I knew that Biddy O'Donnell had discovered television. It was how she was figuring out her new world. While I had

11

sympathy for her, it wasn't going to look good if she kept messing with Karen's TVs.

"*Antiques Roadshow*. It's always the *Antiques Roadshow*."

Even for Biddy O'Donnell, that was a strange choice. I wondered if there really was something wrong in the O'Donnell house's new wiring. "Have you talked to the electrician?"

"The electrician says it's nothing to do with them. If the TV's turning on, that means it's getting electricity all right."

"Maybe the cable provider?"

"No. When I explained the problem, the man on the phone laughed and said maybe I had a ghost."

I laughed, but it was a feeble effort.

While Biddy O'Donnell occasionally paid me a visit, usually with her horrible familiar, Pyewacket, she hadn't been by recently. I thought she was getting quite comfortable in the O'Donnell house. I suspected I'd have to visit her and see if she had a new favorite show. It was easy to find an excuse to visit. "I'm dying to see how the new place is coming along. When can I see it?"

"I'd be thrilled if you'd come over. I can show the place off, and you can help me decide about which antiques to display. I'm displaying some of my father's collections." Her voice softened. She'd only become close to her father late in his life, and she clearly missed him. He'd been an enthusiastic collector of everything from old toys to antique glass, so she had lots of stuff to display for her guests. "I've also got stock from Granny's Drawers, but I don't want to overdo it."

I hadn't thought of that. "So you've essentially got a second store. Will you hang price tags from the furniture and the china?"

She shook her head so hard, her ponytail bounced.

"Nothing so tacky. But there will be a discreet card indicating that all one-of-a-kind items and antiques are available for purchase."

"Nice. Classy."

"Are you teasing me?"

I laughed. "Only a little."

"Why don't you come tonight?"

"I can't wait."

Even though I wanted to have a quiet word with Biddy, I was excited to see what Karen Tate had done with the place. Last time I'd seen it, the beautiful old home had faded with age and some unpleasant things had happened there. But since Karen had inherited the O'Donnell house, she'd turned the place around.

Still, I was going to suggest a smudging ceremony, just to get rid of any remaining bad energy. I knew a smudging ceremony wasn't strong enough to get rid of Biddy O'Donnell, but there was some other old energy that needed cleaning out as well.

I'd made it very clear to Biddy that she was above ground in Ballydehag on probation. If she started causing trouble, she'd have to go back underground. Naturally, the old crone had promised to behave, but I could tell from her beady, crafty eyes that she was wondering, if it came to a fight, which of us was stronger and was probably pretty certain it would be she. I didn't want to put this to the test because I suspected she'd win as well. Still, it was better for both of us if she kept a very low profile. No doubt the guests at the B&B would find a little ghostly activity quirky and charming. But if she went too far, she'd have to go back.

So far, the rest of the coven didn't know that she was still out and about causing trouble. If I had to, I would threaten her with the combined power of me; Kathleen, my sister witch who ran the grocery; and the head of our coven, Pendress Kennedy. Kathleen and I weren't too much of a threat. Pendress looked like Glinda the Good Witch on the outside, but on the inside, she could be as cold and ruthless as Biddy had ever been.

I really hoped we could avoid a war of the witches.

I wondered if I would ever be able to tell Karen Tate that she was also a very distant cousin of mine. She didn't come through the magic side of the family, so she wasn't a witch, but I'd never had extended family. How strange to travel thousands of miles and discover my roots.

Karen was about to leave when there was a bang and a moan from upstairs. She tilted her head and looked startled. "Is there someone upstairs?"

I did my best to look nonchalant. "It's just Cerridwen. That cat seems to use up eight of its nine lives every day, jumping and bonking around up there."

Cerridwen didn't usually groan, but Karen accepted my explanation and said she'd see me later.

When she was gone, I ran upstairs to check on my unwanted writer in residence. I found him grabbing at his hair again, looking petulant. "What's the matter? I told you, you have to be quiet up here. I had a customer in the shop, and you were banging and groaning like a man possessed."

He banged his fist on the desktop, but softly. "I am a man possessed. I'm possessed of a story. But it's hopeless, Quinn. I need to call my researchers. I'm not sure if the missile I'm describing is the Harpoon or the Hellfire."

"Wow. That sounds serious."

"The fate of the world is in my character's hands. And readers care about the technology. I have to get it right. I'm not even sure whether I want active radar homing or GPS."

"Really? I thought you thriller writers made all that weapons stuff up."

He looked as though I'd slapped him with a dead fish. "Make it up? Quinn, I'll have you know that technical detail is one of the hallmarks of my books. My readers would be very upset if I wasn't completely accurate in my research."

"Well, can't you use the internet?" Then I hastily said, "It's not very good here, but at the castle, I know Lochlan Balfour has super high-speed internet. Well, he would, seeing as he owns a tech firm."

Bartholomew sank deeper into my chair. "I can't write there properly. I'm sensitive to atmosphere, you see. And the ambience at Devil's Keep is not good."

I suspected he meant that Oscar Wilde made his life hideous using his extremely sarcastic wit at Bartholomew's expense.

He looked at me hopefully. "Could you phone the United States Department of Defense and find out? I'll give you my list of questions."

"No. I couldn't." Not only did I not have time to be Bartholomew's research assistant, but I'd probably end up on some Homeland Security watchlist.

He looked aggrieved. "Very well. I'll make a list of the books I shall require. You can order them for me."

"This is a bookshop, not a library. I can do that. But you'll have to pay for the books."

"And how do you suggest I do that? Use my credit card? My debit card, perhaps?" His words dripped with sarcasm.

I had no idea how vampires managed to pay for things, but from what I'd seen, cash wasn't an issue. "Don't you have money?"

"I have millions. I just can't get to them." This seemed to be another thing that was irking him.

"Have you talked to Lochlan about it?"

"He says I must be patient. Find something to do that earns money, and over time, savings and property will grow."

"But what are you supposed to do in the meantime?"

He let out a huge sigh. "Exactly."

"Even writing this book, then, won't do anything but flatter your..." I stopped myself before I used the word "ego."

"I may have to take a nom de plume." He looked very sad at the prospect. "They'll bill me as the next Bartholomew Branson. But I don't want to be the next one. I want to be this one."

"It must be really difficult," I said, feeling sympathy for his plight. "But at least you're still around and able to write."

"Cold comfort, Quinn," he said in sepulchral tones. Then he shook his head. "Cold comfort."

I was about to leave him to his cold comfort when he stopped me. "When I've finished writing for the day, we must get busy sending letters and emails about the Irish launch of *Killer in His Sights*. How many copies have you preordered? I should think two hundred would be enough. It's a shame I can't sign them."

Luckily, he didn't stop talking long enough for me to reply, as I hadn't ordered any yet. Two hundred copies? I doubted a small shop in a small Irish village could move half that number, but I decided to order them anyway, knowing I might have to return a lot of unsold copies.

"When you call the publisher, don't let them fob you off. There's a sizable advertising budget, and you're going to require some of it. We'll need plenty of posters for the event. We'd better do those ourselves and some local advertising that we control. But for now, I must get back to my writing."

I went back to the shop, where it was surprisingly busy. I could never work out why a flurry of people would suddenly all decide to go to the bookshop at once. Even accounting for variables like weather and time of day, it seemed random.

However, I managed to find time to order Bartholomew's research books for him. He'd still have to pay, but I decided to sell him the books at my cost.

While I was thinking about Bartholomew and his books, I called my supplier and ordered two hundred copies of *A Killer in His Sights*.

For the launch of an undead author's novel.

What had I dropped myself into?

CHAPTER 3

Since I was bringing a bottle of wine to Karen, I decided to ride my bike up to the O'Donnell house. My route took me past the church where, thanks to a village fundraising effort, the old steeple was being repaired and the church made safe. Behind it I could see the old, gnarled yew tree that had received a most unfortunate haircut, weakening it enough that my ancestor, Biddy O'Donnell, the fearsome and dreaded witch who'd been hanged back in the seventeenth century and buried under that yew, had managed to escape.

I averted my eyes and pedaled on. I was excited to see what Karen had done with the O'Donnell house. I'd seen gardeners at work and some stonemasons outside when I'd driven by a couple of times, but I had not yet been inside.

In my backpack was a bottle of wine for her housewarming and a special gift I'd made myself. A suncatcher, it was an ornament to hang in the window and sparkle when the sun hit it. What Karen wouldn't know was that I'd made it in the shape of the evil eye, using clear quartz and black tourmaline for their protective properties against evil. Then I'd imbued the crystals with extra magic to keep away evil spirits. I considered it like a Biddy repellent.

I knocked very properly on the front door. Karen opened it, her eyes twinkling. I thought she was delighted to be able to show someone around.

"Welcome," she said.

Before I even crossed the threshold, I said, "I can't believe what you've done to the front. It's transformed."

She chuckled, obviously pleased with the compliment. "It's amazing what a team of four strong gardeners can do. Then I had the rock walls fixed and the house repainted. It was desperately in need of some tender, loving care."

She was right. The old girl had cheered right up under a bit of pampering. The garden was tidied, and she'd added new trees and shrubs. There was a sign up outside, and she'd added extra outdoor lighting so the home looked more inviting than I'd ever seen it.

The windows gleamed from a recent cleaning, and the whole place looked cheerful and welcoming where, when I'd been here for Mr. O'Donnell's wake, it had looked dilapidated and tired.

"I'm so happy to show the place off," she said. "Knowing you were coming, I scurried around and got all the new beds made up. Come and see." She'd been much more efficient with her time and resources than I could have imagined in my wildest dreams.

I barely got inside the newly painted front door when she grabbed me.

"Guess what? I've got my first booking next week."

This might be good news for her, but it didn't feel like

very good news to me. I wanted Biddy under control before innocent guests arrived. "Really? So soon?"

"I know. Isn't it grand? I'm excited but nervous as well. I've got everything riding on making a success of O'Donnell House."

I asked her the question that I'd been wondering for a while. "How can you run a bed and breakfast and run your shop at the same time?"

She nodded, her brow wrinkling in concentration. One businesswoman to another. "It's a good question you raise, Quinn. And I've struggled. But if I'm to make a success of both these enterprises, I simply need more help. I've taken out a loan. That will allow me to hire some help in the shop and finish getting the bed and breakfast in tip-top shape."

I didn't like the sound of a loan. I knew from my own experience in The Blarney Tome that nobody was going to get rich running a little shop in Ballydehag. We shopkeepers made what you might call a reasonable living. Enough to buy the essentials of life, but the minute we started paying out wages, the numbers didn't look so good. I knew because I'd done that math myself. More than once. I would love to get some help. But to do it, I would have to earn more money or dip into my savings. And speaking of which...

"Don't you have any savings?"

She laughed. But it wasn't a very amused sound. "I've put every penny I've saved into the O'Donnell renovation. It cost a lot more than I thought, Quinn. I took an online course and learned ever so much. It's the tourists, you see. They expect a certain level of comfort. The prices I could charge for an en suite as opposed to simply a bedroom with a bathroom down the hall was ridiculous. Plus, the Americans won't come if they don't have their own bathroom." She glared at me as though it were my personal fault that Americans were so fussy. She was right, though. Most people I knew, middle-aged Americans, would expect to have their own bathroom. We were long past the hostel stage. When we got up in the middle of the night, we wanted our own facilities.

"But you've only got the one big family bathroom upstairs, haven't you? And was there an en suite off the master?"

"That's right. What I've had to do is take one of the smaller bedrooms and break it into two bathrooms. So now I've got three bedrooms with en suite and two smaller ones that share the family bathroom."

There had been six bedrooms upstairs, and she'd accounted for all of them. "But where will you sleep?"

"I had a small bedroom made when I renovated the kitchen. You remember what a huge room that was."

I nodded. A big, old kitchen that had badly needed renovating last time I'd seen it. "You renovated the kitchen as well. You have been busy."

"You'll have to come and see it. It's beautiful. Walk around with me and let me know if you think anything's missing. You, with your American's eye."

Again, as though I stood in for my entire country. Still, I was dying to see the place. Even more important, if she had guests coming to stay next week, I needed to have a firm word with Biddy O'Donnell. I'd been more than lenient considering the old witch was a distant relative, but I couldn't have her ruining this enterprise that Karen Tate was so excited about. It wasn't just a business, and I understood that. Karen's father hadn't publicly acknowledged her until after his death, when she ended up the beneficiary of his estate.

For her, I knew, this was her way of honoring his legacy. Her late father had been an avid collector, and she had told me she was going to try to theme the rooms around the collections he'd loved the most. I thought it was a great idea. I knew when I stayed in bed and breakfasts, I liked the quirkier ones. Anyone could stay in a soulless chain hotel, but to travel in Ireland and stay in a real family home with personality seemed so much more interesting to me.

Inside, the transformation was dramatic. She walked me around like a tour guide, pointing out what she'd done. "I pulled up all the carpets and had the floors refinished." They were beautiful. Wide plank, original floors. She had big throw rugs that I suspected she'd either bought at auction or had borrowed from Granny's Drawers. They were faded but lovely and perfectly suited the house. The same old sideboard still sat in the big hallway, but it was polished now and held a heavy crystal vase just ready for a bouquet of fresh flowers. The living room that had been so drab and dreary now welcomed me with soft lighting, freshly painted walls and furniture that wasn't new but repurposed. All the woodwork had been polished, the curtains replaced. The big fireplace was ready for a comforting blaze, and a good-size television took up one corner.

The display cabinets that had previously been so crammed with Billy O'Donnell's many collections now high-lighted china, glass, and fresh-polished silver. There was a Victorian tea set complete with china-faced dolls and a sparkling collection of early Waterford crystal.

There was a bookshelf with old and interesting-looking books, some of which she'd bought from The Blarney Tome.

The big dining room, with its table that seated twelve, would be perfect for breakfasts. Again, I remembered the display cabinets as stuffed with everything from old tin toys to china figurines. Now there was space, and she'd displayed collectibles. I peered into a cabinet and said, "This is nice. Very Irish." A whole shelf was dedicated to Belleek, glowing cream-colored porcelain jugs, plates, vases, and dishes embellished with green shamrocks.

"Too much? I've really showcased everything Irish I could find. Belleek and Waterford, and all the linens are Irish. I also have some lesser known Irish potters and silversmiths on display."

"No. I think it's fine. Your visitors can shop for souvenirs to take back home without even leaving the comfort of the B&B."

"That's what I'm hoping. And wait until you see the kitchen."

Like the rest of the house, the kitchen had been completely transformed. Gone were the ancient cupboards and appliances that looked rusty and dangerous. Now she had a big industrial range, a huge, stainless-steel fridge, two dishwashers, a small seating area and a desk that looked out onto the back garden. The kitchen was smaller than I remembered because, as she'd told me, she'd built a bedroom off the kitchen. She took me in, and it was as though she'd run out of money and made her own room as simple as possible. There was nothing in it but a double bed, a dresser, and a cupboard. She'd also put in a small bathroom for herself.

"I hated to do it—what a waste of money—but I can't be

running up the stairs to use the loo. I must come out in the morning freshly showered and dressed and all made up. Can't be running up and down the place in my nightgown."

I agreed that she couldn't.

She took me at last upstairs to see the guest rooms. Each held either a queen-size bed or two singles, and armchairs and dressers that she'd either refurbished or painted white and embellished with new hardware. Once more, she'd chosen pretty china and antiques either from her father's collection or her own and furnished the beds with luxurious linens. The rooms were beautiful, and I told her so. I loved the way she'd mixed the antique and quirky with modern comfort. She was very anxious for my seal of approval on the bathrooms, and I was able to reassure her that they were completely up to my American standards. Each had a shower, sink and toilet and beautiful, thick and luxurious towels. She'd gone high-end with the soaps and lotions. I'd love to stay here, but I suspected I wouldn't be able to afford it.

Each bedroom also had its own television. She said, on a light laugh, "At least the TVs aren't on. Sometimes I walk in and they're all blaring away."

"You really should get that seen to," I said. Though I had a pretty good idea how they were getting turned on. I felt Biddy there, an unseen presence creeping along behind me. I bet if I swung around, I could catch her sliding out of sight. But, of course, I didn't.

Karen showed me the main bathroom last. She'd left the layout the same but changed all the fixtures. Even though the mirror was brand new, this was where Biddy O'Donnell had first made contact with me. I glanced fleetingly into the mirror and caught not only my own reflection but a pale shadow behind me. I'd been right then. The old witch was following along, listening to every word.

I told Karen, honestly, how amazed I was and how beautiful it all looked.

She seemed pleased but anxious too. "Quinn, it's so important to me that this goes well. Especially at the beginning. I'm keeping my rates quite reasonable until I get some nice reviews. I so want my early customers to be happy ones."

"I'm sure they will be. It's absolutely gorgeous." So long as they weren't frightened by an ornery ghost-witch.

She was showing me the final room, what had formerly been the master. "I'll charge the most for this room, as it's got the king-size bed and the en suite has a bathtub as well as the shower."

"It's a lovely room." I was about to ask her what her rates were and offer to carry her brochures in the bookshop when I heard a familiar tune. A striking melody, heavy with brass, and even though I recognized it, it took me a second. Then Karen threw up her hands. "There it goes again. It's the big telly downstairs. Why does it always turn on to *Antiques Roadshow*?"

"I don't know. Let's go down and see." I led the way so I could catch my witchy ancestor in the act. Naturally, the minute I stepped into the living room downstairs, she disappeared so fast there was nothing left but the scent of decay.

Fiona Bruce was smiling from the big TV and welcoming us to some gorgeous manor house. "It's not that I don't love *Antiques Roadshow*," Karen said as she switched the TV off, "but I keep stopping to watch it, and I don't have time to be distracted. Though, yesterday, I discovered that the vase there on the mantel is worth eight hundred pounds in England."

I looked to where she was pointing and saw a pretty vase, dark blue with what looked like clouds and birds on it. "It's early Moorcroft," Karen said. "I had no idea."

"I have a gift for you," I said. I went to my backpack and pulled out the wrapped suncatcher.

She said, "Oh, you shouldn't have," but opened it so eagerly I knew she was pleased.

As she took out the crystal ornament on its silver chain, I felt the power of the spelled stones casting out their protective energy. There was a rude sound from behind me, and Biddy backed off. Good, it was working then.

"You must hang it in the window," I told her. That way, sun and starlight and moonlight would help keep its energy high. On impulse, I said, "I can do you one for every room if you like. They're awfully pretty when the sun hits them."

"No, that's all right. You've done enough. But I'll hang this one here. It's so pretty."

Luckily, there was a bracket in the middle of the window that helped support the curtain rod with the new plum-colored drapes. Karen hung the crystal from it, and even though it was evening, the crystal glowed. I pictured the evil eye glaring at Biddy.

I had to get Karen out of the house because I knew that Biddy wouldn't appear while she was there with me, obviously.

When I pulled out the second item I'd brought along, a bottle of Malbec, she struck a match and lit the fire in the living room. We sat in two of the overstuffed chairs and sipped wine. It was glorious. Cozy and comfortable. She told me she'd contemplated going with a gas fireplace but decided wood was both more authentic and more cheerful. She sighed. "Also a lot more work."

"Are you worried about the amount of work?"

"I'm strong, and I'm used to working hard. There are women in the village I can hire if I need extra help. I'll see how it goes running both of the businesses. At first, of course, the B and B will be slow. If I get very busy, then I might think about renting the shop out to someone else."

We chatted for an hour, and then she said, on impulse, "You know the pub is offering pizza now?"

I felt my jaw drop. "Are you kidding me? That is a luxury I never thought I'd find in Ballydehag." Along with a bagel place, a decent hair salon, Starbucks, and a hundred other conveniences I missed from Seattle.

She giggled. "I know. I think it's ever such a good idea. And the more we support it, the more likely it is to remain."

"Are you suggesting we order a pizza?"

"I am. They don't deliver. I'd have to pick it up. Would you care to join me?"

"I think that's a fabulous idea." Also a great way to get rid of Karen, as I wanted a few minutes alone with Biddy. I shrugged. "I foolishly only brought my bicycle. I didn't think I'd be staying for dinner, otherwise I'd go and collect it."

"No worries. I'll run up and get the pizza. And I'll drive you home later. I don't want you riding around in the dark."

We happily agreed on the pizza with the works, and she went off to fetch it.

The minute the door shut behind her, I stood and put my hands on my hips. I was about to call out to Biddy, but I didn't have to. I heard one of the televisions go on upstairs. What was with that woman and the TV? I ran lightly up the stairs.

The sound was coming from the biggest and most luxurious of the bedrooms. Naturally.

I opened it and went in. Biddy O'Donnell did not improve with age. She did not improve with a closer knowledge of her, either. She looked like a terrifying, old witch from fairy tales. She was lying on the beautiful, new bed with pillows propped up behind her.

She glanced up when I came in. "Very comfortable, these beds. That woman's restless and flighty, but she has made my old home very comfortable."

"Biddy, this hasn't been your home for four hundred years. And anyway, yours burned down. This wasn't built till two hundred years ago."

"Stop arguing about straws, girl. And shut that door. There's a draught."

"Biddy, what are you doing?"

"Shh. Will you look at that, girl? Why, it looks like it's been trodden on."

I followed her gaze to the television screen. One of the antique experts was raving about a small thimble. Biddy was right. The thimble was dented and squashed. It did look like it had been stepped on.

"To find a silver thimble of this age is very unusual. How did you come across it?"

"I was mudlarking in the Thames," said a bearded man who looked bashful, as though he didn't want the viewing public to know he spent his free time sifting through old river mud looking for treasure.

After pointing out various features of the thimble, the antique expert told the bearded man it was worth at least five hundred pounds.

Biddy was beside herself. "Five hundred pounds for something that prevents your thumb from getting pricked? All the old rubbish I used to have around my house is worth a fortune. Do you know what the fools will pay for a tankard like ones I used in my pub?"

My lips twitched in spite of myself. "Quite a bit, I imagine."

Those crafty, cunning, black eyes looked straight at me. "There's fortunes to be made, Quinn. Fortunes."

I was going to argue with her that finding old tankards wasn't going to be easy. That's why they were worth so much now. But even as I opened my mouth to speak, she shushed me. And turned the volume up on the television.

But I wanted her attention. I pointed at the television and turned it off by magic.

Before she could turn it back on, I said, "Biddy, Karen Tate has put a lot of work and money into making this house an inn."

Biddy nodded. "Aye. She's a hard worker. And she's a good eye for business. She's our kin and kith, no mistake."

I was pleased to see that she approved of Karen Tate's enterprise. "Good. You were an enterprising businesswoman in your day too." She had been. She'd run an inn and made a lot of money. Unfortunately, she had a bad habit of marrying men and murdering them, plus putting curses on her enemies, which was how she'd ended up with her unfortunate end.

Her mangy and miserable familiar, Pyewacket, humped beside her on the bed, one suspicious eye open. She turned on me, her head at an odd angle on her paws.

Pyewacket had been hanged too.

"So you're not going to bother the guests? You're not going to ruin Karen Tate's business?"

"No. Why would I? She's made a nice home for me. We'll get on fine."

"But you have to stop turning the television on all the time."

"But I must watch my show. It's how I find out the value of things."

"But even if you could find old tankards and things, how will you sell them?"

She looked at me like I was a dimwit. "What are you? An eejit? On eBay, of course."

CHAPTER 4

I closed my eyes and opened them. "You're a hanged witch. You haven't been alive for hundreds of years. How on earth do you know about eBay?"

"I may be dead, but *I'm* not an eejit. I watch what that girl's doing. She buys things on eBay. Sells them too."

The thought of Biddy O'Donnell as an eBay seller was almost more than I could bear.

"Please, just promise me you won't cause trouble. If Karen has guests, you mustn't put the television on."

She sniffed. "Well, I suppose I shall have to come to you then. How big is your television?"

Oh, the thought of me and Biddy O'Donnell curled up on Friday night watching *Antiques Roadshow,* with our two familiars hissing at each other, made my skin twitch.

"I'll put a television in the upstairs of my shop. You can watch it there."

Those sly eyes flitted my way and then away again. "We'll see."

That sounded ominous, but I didn't have any more time

to chat, as I could hear Karen Tate returning. Besides, I was starving. I couldn't wait to see how the pizza tasted in Bally-dehag, Ireland.

Sean O'Grady ran the local pub and also did catering. "Sean had a brick oven installed," Karen said as we munched on pizza that was as good as any I'd had in the States. "What do you think?"

"I think I want to marry it and have its babies," I said, through a mouthful thick with cheese and oregano-flavored sauce.

She laughed, but we agreed we'd likely be regular partakers of Sean's latest delicacy. "I wonder if I should serve pizza at the book launch," I mused, then told Karen about the gala book launch.

She was very supportive of this event that would bring business to our small village. She wiped a speck of sauce from her lower lip and then said, "And if anyone needs a place to stay..."

Bartholomew Branson was as good as his word. Unfortunately. I had hoped that he would quickly lose interest in organizing a gala launch for his book, a launch he couldn't even attend, but he was made of sterner stuff. His desire to see his last book come to market was stronger than his sadness at not being there. In fact, he invited so many people, they'd never all crowd into my shop.

Lochlan Balfour stepped forward and offered the castle for a gala cocktail party for the launch. We'd have book sales at the shop and then a much bigger party that I realized was going to be a literary wake for the sadly departed author.

The nice thing about moving the big event to the castle was that I didn't have to do so much work. Sean O'Grady agreed to do the catering with the help of the nice, young couple that ran the coffee shop and bistro. This was an event that began to get all of Ballydehag excited. It wasn't often that we had a major event taking place in our sleepy little town. At least not anything the mortals usually knew about.

I couldn't shake the feeling that there might be trouble ahead, but once the event got moving, there wasn't much I could do about it. Bartholomew wrote the emails and the letters that I signed, and we were all getting excited about the big day. I had the front window stocked with all of Branson's thrillers front and center.

I'd tried to keep Bartholomew's expectations from getting overheated. He was so certain he could snap his undead fingers and bring publishing professionals to the literary wilderness, but I wasn't so sure.

"I'll prove you wrong, Quinn," he said. "Have a little faith."

To my shock, he was right. We had Bartholomew's British editor and his British agent coming, as well as key staff from the Dublin publishing office.

They were staying over for a couple of nights at O'Donnell House, so Karen was pretty excited about the event, too.

I'd never known before what a big deal publishing was behind the scenes. It wasn't just a guy delivering a bunch of typed pages and the next thing, a book turned up. There was a lot of marketing and promotions planning that went into supporting a big-name author. I did feel bad for him that he wouldn't have a role in the limelight, but at least at the castle, he'd be able to overlook the event without being seen.

But for the book launch, there was no way he could be here. He'd just have to make do with my firsthand account, and I had promised him I'd take lots of photographs. I drew the line at hiring a camera company to film the entire thing. He tried to argue, but I reminded him that Lochlan would be at the launch, and how would it look when he didn't show up on film?

The day before the launch I spent tidying up the shop so it looked better than it had any time since I'd been here. I made a nice, big space for customers to pick up their copies of *A Killer in His Sights*. Sadly, they couldn't be autographed, and no matter how many awesome strategies Bartholomew came up with, none of them made sense.

Cerridwen was, naturally, very curious at the changes I was making and insisted on rolling over and doing cat acrobatics on the chair I was dragging out of the way when she suddenly flipped to her feet and stared toward the door.

The woman who swept into The Blarney Tome was hard to describe. More than a visual, she was motion and energy and overpowering friendliness. She didn't even look at the books but came straight up to me and said, "Hey there, you must be Quinn Callahan," in a New Jersey accent.

I agreed that I was.

"It's so great to meet you. I'm Candace Branson, but everybody calls me Candy."

She was as sweet as candy too, that kind that sort of sticks in your teeth and makes you feel sick if you eat too much of it.

I must have continued to stare at her, looking stunned.

"Bartholomew Branson's wife. You must have heard of me. I'm so excited about his launch." And then her face went ludicrously sad as though someone had pushed a button. "It was a terrible tragedy. When I lost my Barty."

Bartholomew wasn't my favorite vampire, but had he seriously gone through life being called Barty?

She said, "It's great to have a fellow American here. Let's face it, we're the ones who get things done. Let me know if I can help. I'd be happy to help you organize this thing. The Irish are wonderful people and all, but they're kind of disorganized, if you know what I mean."

Weirdly, I did. It was one of the things I loved about Ireland. The slower pace, not such a focus on money. Well, probably if you were in the Dublin business district it might be as hectic as New York or London; I really didn't know. But out here in Ballydehag, life moved slower. People had more time to stand around and gossip. And if you wanted something done, you had to be prepared to wait. I'd already become so accustomed to the pace that it was a shock to have someone so very American and energetic already offering help when we'd been acquainted all of about a minute and a half.

Still, I wasn't one to turn down help. Although I was quite puzzled to find that Bartholomew Branson had a wife. It was the first I'd heard of it.

"I'm so sorry for your loss," I finally managed. And in so many ways, I wished she hadn't had that loss. My life would sure be easier if I didn't have to balance the egos of Oscar Wilde and Bartholomew Branson.

"Thank you." She sighed deeply. "Barty was the love of my life, and I was his."

I said, "I didn't know he was married."

She laughed, but it was a forced sound. "Honey, we were married for twenty-three years. I couldn't have been happier." She fished around in a large handbag festooned with fake diamonds and pulled out a packet of tissues. One of those that have a slogan on it. Her tissues were bright pink and said *Don't blow it.*

She took one out, and I noticed her manicure was bright purple with sparkles. She dabbed at her eyes. I was impressed, as she barely budged the false eyelashes. Her eyes were a bright, bright blue, her hair frosted blond, and I suspected there were some cosmetic miracles going on to keep her lips that plump and her skin that smooth.

What she didn't know, of course, was that I saw Bartholomew every week. And lately much more frequently. He had never once mentioned a wife, and Bartholomew Branson was not a reticent man. He was only too happy to tell us all about the things he missed. All the trappings of celebrity. The five-star hotels, the eager fans who sent him glowing emails and gifts. The rich person's lifestyle. In none of these sad stories that he related about the past was there ever a Mrs.

Not my business.

She said, "When Barty's agent told me about this event, I thought it was just darling. And since my poor, sweet Barty passed away off the shores of Ireland, it seemed perfectly fitting to me that his book should be published and launched here. And I'm only too happy to be involved. After all, I'm all that's left of poor Barty now." She put a hand with sparkling, purple nails to her chest.

If only that were true.

But that was unkind. He might be really annoying, but it wasn't his fault he'd been turned into a vampire in the middle of a celebrity cruise. That would bum anybody out.

"I was thinking, Barty always used to love book signings. And the poor fans who will show up for a hardcover copy fresh off the press should get something special. How would it be if I signed them?"

The force of her personality and the torrent of words coming at me made me take a step back until I was pressed against the wall of books. I knew one thing. If anybody was going to decide who was signing his books, it should be Bartholomew himself, and I wouldn't be offering her anything until I talked to him. So I shrugged and said, "It's really not my call. I guess the publishers will have to decide."

For the first time, her bright friendliness dimmed a watt or two. "Well, his agent thought it was a great idea."

"Sure. It is a great idea. It's just not my call to make."

She gazed at the big poster Bartholomew had hung behind my cash desk. "So tell me everything you've got organized. I used to host a lot of parties. And, of course, nobody knows better than I do what Barty would have liked."

I had to argue with her there. I thought "Barty" had some very strong ideas about what he wanted. And I'd be taking his instructions before hers. Especially as Barty had done so much to make his event happen.

Still, she'd come a long way, so I indulged her. "We'll have the books here to buy, then the event moves to Devil's Keep. That's the big castle at the edge of town. There will be drinks and snacks and some speeches."

She nodded. "It won't be the same without Barty there. I'm glad I followed my instinct and jumped on a plane to get right over here." She glanced at the poster. "Too bad it's too late to put my picture on the posters."

"Yes. What a shame."

"Never mind. I've got a couple of media interviews scheduled."

"Really?" Bartholomew had been pretty clear about what he wanted. If his wife was so eager to be involved, why had he never mentioned her?

She said, "I have a big secret of my own. I can't wait to tell everybody." She wagged her finger at me like we were co-conspirators. "I'll have a little announcement at the launch party."

For a terrible moment, I wondered if she'd somehow caught a glimpse of Bartholomew, who did have a bad habit of wandering around when he really shouldn't. Ballydehag was remote enough that after the publicity had died down from his recent drowning, there wasn't too much chance that he'd be recognized on the street. But with the launch, his picture was everywhere again, and besides, who would know him better than his wife? But then I realized she wouldn't be making a surprise announcement if she'd caught sight of her dead husband. She'd be getting hold of the police or a private investigator or a psychic. So my rapid heartbeat settled a bit.

We looked at each other, and she clearly expected me to say something. Out of politeness more than genuine interest, I said, "Do you have a place to stay tonight?"

She brightened up again. The friendly breeziness was back. "Oh, yes. The most darling little bed and breakfast. It's just opened here in Ballydehag. All of us are staying there."

For some reason, I felt a shiver of dread go down my spine. "You're staying at the O'Donnell House?"

"That's right. I just checked in before I came here. And as I said, it's absolutely darling. Since I'm sort of the guest of honor, the nice lady who runs it gave me the best bedroom, the one at the front of the house."

I felt my smile going rigid on my face as though someone had Botoxed it into place.

"The front bedroom."

That was where Biddy seemed to spend a lot of her time. Like Candace "call-me-Candy" Branson, Biddy O'Donnell also liked to settle herself in the best room in the house. Karen's only fear when she'd told me the publishing execs were staying in O'Donnell House was that the electrical problem still hadn't been solved. "What'll I do if these posh men from London find their televisions play nothing but the *Antiques Roadshow*?"

"I'm sure they'll be too busy with the launch to watch TV," I soothed her, hoping that was true.

I wondered how this was going to turn out, Biddy and Candy sharing a room. I was grateful for one thing. Bartholomew wasn't working upstairs today. If he had been, he'd have no doubt been tempted to run down and see his wife. I had to go and warn him she was here. I hadn't seen her name on the guest list. I suspected her presence was going to give him a shock.

And me another gray hair.

"Well, I'd better get going," she said. Then she pulled out her mobile phone. "Just put your details into my phone, honey, would you? We should keep in touch."

I didn't know how to refuse.

After Candace left, I finished my preparations, but my mind was in turmoil. I had a strong intuition that I needed to tell Bartholomew that his widow was wandering around town. However, I couldn't just close up at three o'clock in the afternoon because I felt like it. Still, if the wife was wandering around town, Bartholomew Branson had to be kept hidden away.

With no other options, I phoned Lochlan Balfour. Even though he ran a super successful company, whenever I phoned him, he picked up right away. "Quinn. How's the planning going?"

It seemed to be the question we all had for each other these days. I said, "Something interesting happened. Bartholomew Branson's wife showed up."

There was a tiny beat of silence. "His wife. That seems surprising."

"I thought so too. He never talks about her. Do you think you should warn him?"

"I think you should come over here and tell him yourself. He may want to know how she looked, what conversation passed between you. Things I can't tell him."

"I can't. It's three o'clock in the afternoon. I don't close the shop until five."

"Can't you hire some extra staff? Especially now, we need you here."

As flattered as I was that they wanted my help and expertise at the castle, I had a shop to run. Which I explained to him. "And I can't afford to pay staff. The bookstore can barely support me as it is."

"Give me a minute. I'll wake up Lady Cork and send her along to help."

Was he having me on? "Lady Cork dresses like she's still in the 1800s. And she's a kleptomaniac," I reminded him.

"All right. It will have to be Dierdre then. Though she's been very helpful hanging posters and keeping Branson and Wilde apart."

I had another, even stronger objection. "Are you sure I can trust a vampire to run a shop catering to humans?"

"I'll make sure she's fed before she comes," he said, as though that were the only problem.

"But won't the townspeople wonder about the strange and rather pale woman who's suddenly selling them books?"

"First, it's Ireland. Everyone's pale. And second, she's not unknown. Unlike Bartholomew Branson, Dierdre's able to mix with the villagers."

"I don't know." I was worried that this would all go wrong.

"And you wouldn't have to pay her."

Well, that clinched it. "Okay. Put Lady Cork between the warring authors and send Dierdre to me." Dierdre wasn't the most exciting person, dead or alive, but she dressed in time-less Chanel-style suits rather than hoop skirts and could be counted on not to steal things.

I tidied up the shop, and when my new undead assistant arrived, I quickly explained to her how the cash register worked and left her to it. Cerridwen stared down at the vampire from the top of a bookshelf and then jumped down and took herself upstairs, no doubt for a well-earned nap.

I took my bike and cycled to the castle. It didn't take me very long. I always loved coming here. It was like getting to go inside a major tourist attraction with no other tourists. It made me feel special. Connected.

I walked in and found a hub of activity.

Sean O'Grady was setting up food stations and preparing the bar. Thomas Blood and a vampire I didn't know were hanging posters from the old stone walls. Apart from the promotional ones, Bartholomew had commissioned some that had quotes from his books. Since Oscar Wilde was currently reading one while holding a handkerchief to his mouth as though holding back vomit, I wasn't sure he'd done himself any favors.

Bartholomew was looking over the guest list. He had a smile on his face, so it must be good news. When he saw me, his smile widened. "Quinn. Excellent work. Nearly everyone of any importance has said yes to your invitation."

Since we both knew the invitations had come from him and just had my name on them, I could honestly say, "But that's all because of you. These are your colleagues and fans. Congratulations."

I'd said exactly what he'd wanted me to, of course, and he beamed with pleasure.

"And what can I do for you today, Quinn? I can't wait until the first books arrive. You'll have one of the only print copies ever actually signed by the author himself."

Oh, that was a perfect segue into what I had to tell him. I thanked him profusely for the honor, even though it meant I'd have to hide that book away forever. "I had a surprise visitor today."

"Oh, yes? One of my rabid fans, no doubt?"

"No."

"Don't tell me. My New York publisher decided to come after all?"

"No. It was your wife."

His face went from pleased to the opposite so fast, it was ludicrous.

"What wife?" he demanded in a tone that did not suggest

all was sunshine and roses with him and Candace "call-me-Candy."

"She introduced herself as Candace Branson. Candy."

He banged the guest list down on a handy table that would hold appetizers tomorrow night. "Oh, that scheming, lying, conniving—"

"Do we assume you and your wife aren't on the best of terms?" Lochlan Balfour interrupted him smoothly.

"On the best of terms? That woman's a monster. She divorced me and took me for everything I had."

"Not everything, I'm guessing," I said, having heard about his luxurious lifestyle.

He turned to me and scowled. "Millions, Quinn. That woman cost me millions."

"She made it sound like you were happily married."

"Maybe for the first year or two. And then my success came so quickly, and suddenly there was all this money and..."

He got a slightly guilty look on his face, and I had a feeling I knew where this was going. "And you cheated on her."

His scowl deepened. "She cheated on me first."

"So, not the loving couple she described then."

"I haven't spoken to that honey badger in three years. She hired shark lawyer after shark lawyer to make sure she got bigger and bigger alimony payments. She was ravenous for cash. Insatiable."

"Well, she's also here. And she had this great idea that she should sign your books on your behalf."

"Over my dead body!" he bellowed.

There was a terrible silence.

He let out a pent-up breath of frustration. "I keep forgetting."

"What are we going to do?" I asked everyone in the room, since they'd all abandoned whatever they'd been doing and had come closer to listen.

Bartholomew glanced around. "We'll have to get rid of her."

CHAPTER 5

I left the castle feeling even more perturbed about the upcoming literary event than I had before discovering Bartholomew's ex-wife was on the scene and Bartholomew was far from pleased about it. I was pedaling back to the shop when my phone rang. I pulled over and answered it, not wanting to topple off my bike in the middle of a phone conversation, and discovered it was Candace Branson, of all people. She was as friendly as before.

"Quinn, I was talking to Giles Montague, that's Barty's editor, and their darling PR girl, Chloe, and his agent is here too. Philip. We thought it would be a good idea for us to have a meeting tonight to make sure we're all on the same page." She let out a long sigh. "I only wish that Barty could be here."

And Barty only wished Candace was thousands of miles away. Still, there wasn't much I could do. If Bartholomew's agent and editor were happy to accept her involvement in the book launch, I was in no position to turn her down. I agreed to meet them at the bed and breakfast at seven that evening.

When I got to O'Donnell House, I thought the meeting

had already started. I heard voices coming from Karen Tate's front room. Karen let me in, looking both thrilled and harassed. "I can't believe it. Practically my first guests. These are really important people, Quinn. And they chose my bed and breakfast."

I was as encouraging as I knew how to be. It was a gorgeous spot, and I knew she would be an excellent host. So long as Biddy stayed in check, she'd be fine.

She shook her head. "If I could just work out whatever's wrong with the televisions."

My jaw clenched like one of Bartholomew's heroes fighting the forces of evil. I was going to have to do something about Biddy.

I explained that I was here to meet with the publishing people, and she told me to go right in. I walked into the living room and found five people sitting around watching the TV. Naturally, *Antiques Roadshow* was playing.

A thin man in a three-piece suit who I was positive must be Giles Montague said, "My parents used to have a sideboard like that. Old rubbish, I thought it was. And look at that. I could have got seven hundred quid at auction, according to them."

I cleared my throat, and everyone turned to me. Candace rushed up and gave me a hug, which seemed a bit over the top, seeing as we'd only just met. Then she turned, her arm still around me as though we were the best of friends. "This is Quinn Callahan, everybody. She runs that darling little shop called The Blarney Tome. I giggled my head off when I first saw the name of your bookshop. That's so quaint. So Irish."

I smiled in a feeble way, and Candace enthusiastically— because she did everything enthusiastically—introduced me to the other people in the room. I had been correct that the man in the three-piece suit was Giles Montague, Bartholomew's London editor. He rose and came forward. He was much taller than me and quite slender. His silver hair was perfectly coiffed, and he wore glasses with gold frames.

He reached for my hand. "I've heard so much about you. I'm sure I speak for all of us when I say that Bartholomew Branson would have been so pleased to have known that a small shopkeeper in the wilds of County Cork had such a passion for his work that she could make an event like this happen."

If only he knew. I tried to look like someone who was passionate about Bartholomew Branson's work, which wasn't easy. Fortunately, he didn't expect me to gush over the late writer's works. He in turn introduced me to Chloe Lynch. She was probably in her late twenties, sleek and elegant with long, red hair and cool green eyes. She had a tablet computer in her hands. "We're very excited. The books have arrived by truck. They'll be delivered first thing tomorrow. This should get excellent press. Which will boost book sales."

"Not that that will do Bartholomew Branson much good," I reminded them all.

They all glanced at his ex-wife. "No."

What did that weird glance mean? Was the ex-wife Branson's beneficiary? How curious, since they'd been divorced when he died, and from what he'd said, she wasn't someone he loved giving his money to. I supposed he'd been so in the fullness of life that it hadn't occurred to him to change his will. But if he was as angry at his ex-wife as he seemed to be, it was odd that he hadn't. Well, again, none of my business.

"And this is Philip Hazeltine. Barty's London agent. Even

though Barty was an American, it was Philip who first took him on as a client and then sold his first book to Giles, so they have history," Candy explained.

"How do you do?" Philip asked in an accent that was excessively proper and British. He sounded like one of the royal family. He was dark-haired, a little overweight, but smooth and urbane. He also shook my hand.

"I'm very well, thank you," I replied, equally polite.

"Quinn Callahan. What a pleasure to meet a bookseller. One so rarely has a chance to venture out into the farther reaches of literary fandom."

Was this guy for real? "I'm so glad you could make it," I said.

The final person in the room was a flashy-looking, chubby, balding man who Candace introduced as, "My friend Irving Schulz. Irving came with me to support me on the journey. It's such an emotional thing, coming here to where my Barty was last seen alive." She reached for that pack of tissues I had seen earlier and dabbed once more at her eyes. "It's been so wonderful to have someone I could lean on."

"Happy to be of service," he said, looking fondly on Candace. "That's what friends are for."

Philip Hazeltine was looking at them with a skeptical eye. "How exactly do you two know each other?" he asked.

Candace shut her handbag with a snap. "We've known each other for years. I hardly remember how we met. In literary circles, you meet a lot of people."

"I was a big fan of Branson's," Irving Schulz said, spreading his hands as though describing a fish he'd caught. "Big fan."

Interestingly, he was the only person in the room who had admitted to being a fan of the thriller author's.

We went over once more how the event would proceed, and then Giles Montague said, "I have a little gift for you. You mustn't show anyone. This is completely top secret and under wraps until tomorrow."

And like a magician, he pulled forth Bartholomew Branson's brand-new book in hardcover. In spite of myself, I was thrilled. I must be one of the first people in the world to see the novel in print. I thanked him and promised that I would treasure it.

The cover showed a tough-looking guy with a gun in his hand and a military base behind him. "You see the way the title's embossed."

"Yes. It looks great."

"And you've printed Barty's name in nice, big letters. That was always so important to him," Candace offered. "Number one *New York Times* Bestselling Author," she read as though this might be news to any of us.

"Do you want me to autograph it for you, honey?" Candace asked.

"That's okay."

"I know you asked for two hundred copies," Chloe said in her businesslike way. "But we made it three hundred to be safe."

"I'd be thrilled to sell three hundred hardcovers," I said. There'd be enough for everyone who came in person to pick up a book at the launch, and I'd also agreed to ship books out from The Blarney Tome to anyone who couldn't make the event.

"Will you look at that?" Irving suddenly said, in a voice of amazement. "My Aunt Betty had a doll like that. I think she gave it to Goodwill." We all watched as the appraiser talked about dolls from the 1930s. I excused myself, saying I had a lot to do before tomorrow, and left them all glued to the TV.

I headed straight home to find Cerridwen looking miffed and standing expectantly beside her empty bowl.

"I'm sorry I'm late," I said, immediately rushing to get her food. As much as I wanted to kick back and put my feet up because it was going to be a long day tomorrow, I couldn't. I kept looking at that book sitting on my kitchen counter, and I knew that the person who would really be excited to see it was at the castle.

Poor Bartholomew, he'd had such a shock finding out that his ex-wife had pushed her way into the launch that I thought the least I could do was take him a copy of his brand-new book hot off the press.

Of course, this wasn't my usual kind of a read. The front cover was a bit garish with lots of red and yellow. *A Killer in His Sights* was in black, in an aggressive font, and in slightly smaller black letters the tagline read, "A secret government agency taught him how to kill; now they want to kill him."

I flipped the book over and read the short biography of Bartholomew on the back cover. I felt a little bit sad at the final line, which was that the famous author had disappeared off the coast of Ireland while on a cruise.

Well, I knew where the mysterious author was, and I knew how very pleased he'd be to see the first copy of his book. So, having assuaged Cerridwen's hunger, I grabbed myself a quick dinner and headed off to the castle.

All was still hustle and bustle at Devil's Keep. Bartholomew was determined that everything should be perfect. He'd clearly worn the other vampires and the staff at the castle to a frazzle with his demands. But he'd achieved what he'd wanted to. Huge posters of his book cover hung from the massive high ceilings, and he had pictures of all his book covers and various pictures of himself. Here he was shaking hands with a former president of the United States. Here he was with his arm around a hot, young actor who had starred in the film version of one of his books. Here he was looking off into the desert as though scanning for enemies. He'd become as much of a character as his fictitious heroes.

"Bartholomew, it looks amazing," I told him.

He looked pleased to see me. "At least someone has an eye for promotion. Thank you, Quinn, for your good taste."

"I have really good news. I brought you a present," I said, hardly able to keep the excitement from my voice. I knew how much this book meant to him. From behind my back I pulled *A Killer in His Sights* and presented it to him. His face lit with excitement.

"Oh, they've done a very good job. I was worried, without me to oversee things. Publishers can be sloppy, you know."

He looked over the front cover happily. "Embossed title. Nice. That costs a few bucks." Turned it over to examine the back. He glanced up at me. "I always worry about the back-cover copy. I had final approval. I insisted on it as one of the terms of my contract. But with this book, I had no input at all. I hope they didn't screw it up."

He began to read, and then the most ludicrous change came over his face. From joy to—I couldn't name the emotion that suffused his face. It was a combination of rage, grief, and disbelief, but mostly rage. Then he made a sound that was again difficult to describe. A howl mixed with a growl mixed with a scream would probably be closest to describe the unearthly sound that came out of him.

Everybody stopped what they were doing to stare. Oscar Wilde plucked the book from his nerveless fingers and, after perusing the back cover of the novel, began to chuckle. Oh, that couldn't be good. The only thing that could make Oscar Wilde this happy would be to see the extremely successful and far less talented writer humiliated.

"What is it?" I cried, unable to bear the suspense.

Oscar Wilde said in his drawl, "This is quite a book you've written here. '*A Killer in His Sights.* A top-secret government agency taught him how to kill. Now they want to *kiss* him.' I think you might have created a whole new genre, my friend. The military conspiracy romance."

CHAPTER 6

"*O*h, no," I cried, as we all stood there in shock. "Are you sure?"

"See for yourself." Oscar handed me the book, and quickly, I read the line. Even worse than the horrible typo was that they'd bolded that line to bring attention to it. "It says kiss instead of kill," I said as though everyone present hadn't figured that out by now.

I looked to Lochlan Balfour, who was the kind of man who could always solve problems. Even big ones. But he stood taking in the scene, shaking his head.

Bartholomew was rousing himself from his shock. "I'm going to *kiss* them. I'm going to go down there and kiss them all, vampire-style. How could they do this to me?" he yelled.

I'd never seen him like this. He looked like a dangerous, undead, blood-sucking vampire. His teeth gnashed. "I'll look like a buffoon."

"You'd think he'd be accustomed by this point," Oscar said, but softly so only I could hear him. Even he must realize that Bartholomew Branson was extremely dangerous in his current state.

"Is there anything you can do?" I asked the furious author. "Maybe they could reprint the book."

"Not in time for the launch." He was pacing and pulling at his hair. "It's tomorrow. This is a disaster."

"Oh, I'm so sorry." How I wished now that I hadn't brought the book with me. All his pleasure in the event was destroyed.

"My career is ruined. Ruined!"

"Calm down," I said. "It's not the whole book, it's only the dust jacket. I'm going to phone the editor right away." I didn't tell him the man was already in Ballydehag in case I incited murder. "Or should I call your agent?"

"Both of them," he yelled. He stomped right up to me. His breathing was really heavy for a vampire. "Tell them the book covers have to be reprinted. Immediately."

I doubted the publisher could reprint the dust jacket that fast. Surreptitiously, I slipped the jacket off the book to see if we could give people the denuded book, but without its bright cover, *A Killer in His Sights* looked awfully dull.

Behind Bartholomew, Lochlan Balfour made a gesture that I was fairly certain meant *make the phone call somewhere else*. Great idea. If I called from here, Bartholomew might grab the phone away from me and yell at them himself. That was the mood he was in. So I waved my phone around theatrically and said, "The cell phone reception here is terrible. I'll go outside and make the call."

"You come right back in, Quinn, the second you're done. And don't you let them talk you out of getting satisfaction. I will not allow that launch to go ahead with a spelling mistake like that."

"I'll do my best."

I left the castle, and Lochlan followed. "What a complete disaster," I said as soon as we were outside. "I never would have brought that book over if I'd known."

"He had to find out sometime. At least this way, maybe there's something we can do."

"But what? There's no way they can reprint thousands of covers before tomorrow."

"I have an idea."

"You do?" Lochlan had been alive so long, he must have faced his share of business setbacks. He seemed like a very resourceful guy.

"You're right, of course. They'll have to reprint all the dust jackets, but for tomorrow, we only need a few hundred."

"Right." Which might as well have been a few million, the way I looked at it.

He stopped me before I could make the phone call. "Let me call a printer friend I know. I have an idea that we could do a small print run of a few hundred collector copies for tomorrow. Give the initial readers the special treatment since they won't have the book signed by the author."

"But your friend would have to work all night," I reminded him.

He gave me a funny look. "I don't think that would be a problem. He usually works at night."

Right. His undead printer.

THERE WAS something very exciting about a book launch. Maybe because I was a real newbie in the bookselling business, it seemed so thrilling. I'd come to love my little shop and the thousands of stories within it. I could guess a lot about people's personalities from the kind of books they were drawn to, and I'd discovered the job suited me.

But this? Offering a brand-new book to the world was beyond anything I'd ever experienced. First of all, my little shop had never been so packed with customers. I'd worried that being so far from a major city, we wouldn't get many people. Especially since they couldn't meet the author. But Bartholomew Branson had some really loyal fans, and they'd driven a long way to be the first ones to receive the first edition of his last book.

Thanks to the overnight rush print job and some creative thinking, even if they weren't getting a signed first edition, these loyal fans were getting something really special. A collector dust jacket. Lochlan had not only had new jackets printed, but there was some extra wording indicating that the book had been purchased at The Blarney Tome and the books had been numbered, a bit like a limited-edition print.

I'd put the exciting news on my website late the night before, and Lochlan had been quick to get the message spread on social media. I'd come in this morning to requests from Branson fans all over the world for one of the collector copies.

Customers who bought the books in person were excited to find out whether they would get copy number 101 or 307. After frantic calls between me, Philip, Giles, and Chloe, we'd agreed to a limited-edition collector's run of five hundred copies. I'd be getting another shipment of books.

Everybody involved was relieved to solve the disaster of the spelling mistake and actually turn it into something positive, no one more so than the poor author.

Since he obviously wasn't able to come to the launch, I hoped he was managing to while away the time at the castle until the event moved over there.

Candace had pouted at first at not being allowed to sign her ex-husband's books, but she seemed to have recovered enough to go around talking to people and very much acting as though she helped write the novel. I walked past her telling some poor soul, "I was his muse, you see." I tried not to roll my eyes.

The event was going so well, I thought that the disastrous mistake on the dust jacket had turned out to be a blessing in disguise, one of those things that seemed like a disaster and then we were able to turn it to our good, mostly because of Lochlan Balfour and his printer friend. Now, instead of just getting a brand-new book, the people that had bothered to come all the way to The Blarney Tome were getting a genuine collector's edition. Bartholomew was delighted, and frankly, so was I. Since Lochlan had made sure that The Blarney Tome got a mention, I suspected that good things might come to me because of this. Maybe I'd forever be known as the Bartholomew Branson store. I suppose there were worse things that could happen to a person.

I'd hired Katie O'Leary, a local teacher and one of my best bookstore customers, to run the cash register so I was free to wander around my fairly small quarters and chat to people. A lot of locals, my regular customers, were in here, and I didn't want them to feel slighted as I fussed over people who'd come from far away and were very unlikely to buy another book here. A lot of them had also been invited to Lochlan's castle afterwards for the celebration, which I thought was a nice touch. Father O'Flanagan, the vicar, made an appearance and looked thrilled with the special copy. "Look, Quinn, they've even mentioned your bookshop. Well done."

Dr. Milsom came in and nodded to me before getting in line to get his own copy. The doctor normally only read fishing books, so I appreciated that he was supporting a local event.

I was really pleased I'd had the foresight to order in extra copies of all Bartholomew's releases from the last five years and even a few copies of the older ones. I had them stacked on a couple of long tables, and there was a steady stream of customers depleting my Branson stock, which warmed my shopkeeper's heart.

I kept glancing at a young man who was standing at the table perusing Branson's older titles. He looked unkempt and needed both a shave and a haircut. He had a backpack hanging from his shoulders that looked like it had seen better days. It also looked like it would hold quite a few books if he chose to sneak them in there when no one was looking. That was why I had my eye on him. As far as security went in this shop? I was it.

So far, all he'd done was stand there, reading one of the books while actual customers had to go around him. He could have been in his own home for all the notice he paid. I suspected he was a poor student. He had that kind of focus about him. But why would a student be here? I didn't recognize him, so he probably wasn't local. One of the cornerstones of security is making sure that anybody dodgy knows you have your eye on them. Besides, my curiosity was growing by the minute, so I went up to him.

"You sure seem to be a Branson fan," I said.

He glanced up, startled as though I had interrupted him in a very private activity. He wore glasses that he pushed back on his nose with one finger and regarded me with cool, gray eyes.

"I guess you could say that," he said in an accent just like mine. I was so used to hearing Irish that having both Candace and this new guy in town with their very fresh American accents felt like old home week.

I said, as expats do everywhere when they meet someone from their own country, "Where are you from?"

"Cleveland." I thought he wanted to go back to his book but, overcome by politeness, he asked, "And you?"

"Seattle."

Well, that was the end of that conversation. I nodded to the book in his hands. "I ship internationally if you're interested." *Hint, hint, maybe you'd like to buy it before you get your dirty fingerprints all over the whole book.*

He laughed. It was a strange sound, not amused at all. "I probably know this book better than you know Seattle." Such a curious statement.

Okay, now he was intriguing me. "You figure?"

He handed me the book. "Open it to any page. Read a sentence, and I can tell you what's going on."

I glanced around the shop. Nobody seemed to need me, and now my interest was caught. I took the book from his hands. There was dirt under his nails. For someone who loved Bartholomew Branson so much, he hadn't exactly treated this gala with a lot of respect. No matter how poor he was, he could have washed his hands.

I glanced at the title. *Behind the Target.* I knew from the Branson catalog that this was a recent title, though not the most recent.

I flipped to a point about halfway through the book and read aloud, "Blake shoved the Russian agent with his hip. He toppled over the stairway. Seven stories was a long way to fall."

Before I could read the next line, the young man recited it. "There was a sound like an egg cracking when the agent hit the marble floor."

I stared.

My new friend said, "That's the spot where John Blake barely gets out of Russia with his life." He put his head back and forth as though he were considering. "That happens to him a lot. Try again."

I'd been skimming ahead, and sure enough, he was right.

I flipped ahead another fifty pages or so. I read, "The meeting was supposed to be a debriefing, but it told him that someone high up in government was scared. Very scared."

"Now he's back in Washington. He's had a private meeting with the president's top security advisor, and now he has to steal a brand-new, previously unheard-of weapon right out from under the arms dealer's nose."

"Wow, you really do know these books. Have you always been a fan?" I was going to have to tell Bartholomew about this unlikely fan. In fact, I was going to invite this kid to the gala. The author should at least get a glimpse of such a passionate fan.

However, to my surprise, the young guy laughed bitterly. "About eight months."

"Really? I'm like that with some authors. I discover them and then I have to read everything they've ever written."

He gave me a tight smile. "Something like that."

"Listen, after this, there's a launch party at Devil's Keep."

He looked startled. "Where?"

I laughed. "I know, it sounds like someplace John Blake would have to sneak into and steal the horns off the devil or something. But it's the castle on the edge of town. It's owned by tech billionaire Lochlan Balfour."

For the first time, he looked enthusiastic. "Cool. I'll definitely drop by."

"Be sure you do."

I wanted Bartholomew to at least see he was gaining some younger fans. He might be undead, but his ego was alive and thriving.

CHAPTER 7

*B*y the time the bookshop event wound down, I was thrilled to see that all five hundred copies of the book were sold or spoken for. I even had a small list of people who'd asked that I send them the regular book when it arrived.

I heaved a sigh of relief and only wished there were more Bartholomew Branson launches to be had because tonight's event had done no end of good to my little shop's bottom line.

However, I doubted that Ballydehag in County Cork was ever going to be a highlight of the literary circuit. Still, it had been fun.

The party then moved to Devil's Keep, and Lochlan Balfour had managed to make the usually dark and forbidding castle seem bright and welcoming. The party was held in the huge gallery, and small groups of people stood chatting and enjoying the champagne, the scotch, the wine and hors d'oeuvres Sean and his helpers were serving. I did my best to mix and mingle myself. But I found that most of the literary types already knew each other. And most of them were talking shop.

Candace Branson seemed a lot more comfortable with shoptalk than I was. I supposed in the time she'd lived with her husband, she'd come to know the book business pretty well.

I knew Bartholomew was watching. I could feel his intense gaze. I hoped he was enjoying himself even though he couldn't party with his fans. Everyone seemed to be having a good time, and lots of people paused to look at the various pictures of him. I overheard several sharing anecdotes about him or talking about which of his books was their favorite and why.

The young man who'd known Bartholomew's books so well walked in and looked around as though he couldn't believe his eyes. It was a common reaction to first seeing Devil's Keep. The place was amazing. It managed to marry medieval with high tech and somehow pull it off. He stood looking around, and I knew instinctively that he didn't know anyone here so I went up to him.

"Hi. Glad you could come."

"Hi. This is quite a place."

He glanced down at his grubby jeans and boots. "Sorry, I forgot my tux in Cleveland."

"That's okay. Any fan of Bartholomew Branson's is welcome. I forgot to ask your name."

"Tristan Holt."

"I'm Quinn Callahan. But you probably knew that." We shook hands anyway. "What brings you to Ballydehag?" I asked. "I'm guessing you didn't fly all the way in from Cleveland just to buy a book that couldn't even be signed by the author."

"I did fly here for Bartholomew Branson, but that's a long story."

It flickered across my mind that maybe this guy was undead and, through some vampire network I knew nothing about, had managed to make contact with a writer he admired. I looked at him objectively. He was certainly pale. It's hard to explain, but once you've been around enough vampires, you get a sense of their inner, extraordinary strength. Tristan Holt just looked way too much like a normal American guy in his twenties who probably spent too many late nights studying or playing video games.

"What do you do in Cleveland?"

"I'm a writer."

Ah. Now it made sense. "You want to be a thriller writer?"

He raised his eyebrows. "Well, I hear there's an opening."

I had to stifle my giggle. I doubted Bartholomew could hear what we were saying, but he'd be so hurt if he thought I was laughing at him behind his back.

"The bar's open," I told him. "Help yourself."

"Don't mind if I do." And he headed off towards a table where Irish whiskey was being lavishly poured. Naturally, most of the publishing executives were already tucking in. Perhaps Tristan Holt could strike up a conversation with one of the agents. Though he'd have helped his cause if he'd cleaned up a bit.

While I was watching Tristan, Lochlan walked up and said, "You must have invited that scrubby chap. I certainly didn't."

"He's a fellow American. Seems to be a Branson fan. You don't mind, do you?"

He shook his head. "You can invite anyone here you like."

Andrew Milsom walked over then, holding a glass of whiskey, which he raised to Lochlan. "That's a fine whiskey you're pouring strangers."

Lochlan laughed. "What's the point of having the means if you don't use them?"

"I like the way you think." Then Andrew turned to me. He was around fifty and the most eligible middle-aged bachelor in Ballydehag. Not that he had a lot of competition. At least, not among the living. "And what a fine evening for you, Quinn. I'd say you've made a few euros tonight."

"I did."

Lochlan walked away to greet a new arrival. He was an excellent host.

"You also helped put Ballydehag on the map," Andrew went on. "Brilliant idea having the collector's edition dust jacket."

I laughed and then leaned closer. "You cannot tell a single soul what I'm about to tell you."

He raised his eyebrows at that. "I've heard plenty of deathbed confessions, believe me. Any secret you've got will be safe with me."

I suspected that was true. He was solid, dependable. A man you could trust. So I told him the whole story of the horrible spelling mistake. He enjoyed it as much as I'd known he would, laughing heartily. "What a good job the poor author's dead. Or it would have killed him."

My laugh was a little too hearty. "You're right."

I saw that he was still carrying his copy of Bartholomew's

new book. "Are you a fan?" I couldn't recall that he'd ever bought a thriller in my shop. "Or supporting the local economy?"

"This is the biggest event we've had in Ballydehag since the church steeple was struck by lightning. I didn't want to miss it."

"The steeple looks great now, though, doesn't it?" I said, not without pride. Between us, Karen Tate and I had donated a couple of valuable objects that helped raise most of the money to repair the old steeple.

He nodded. "Aye, it does. I thought it would be years before they raised enough money, but there was an anonymous bequest."

"That's nice."

He looked uncomfortable. "People think it was me. But it wasn't. More likely it was Lochlan Balfour, who could buy all of Ireland, I should think, if he'd a mind to."

Nobody guessed the money had come from me and Karen, which was fine by both of us. I shrugged. "You heard what Lochlan said. He's got the means. Maybe he decided to use it for the good of the town."

He glanced over at Lochlan, who was busy talking to somebody. "Perhaps."

I thought we'd better move away from that subject, so I asked him if he'd done any fishing lately.

"I'm planning a weekend away. Going to Scotland for some fly-fishing."

Well, that sounded thrilling.

I'd sort of run out of conversation when there was a ruckus.

"How dare you?" Candace Branson shrieked. I glanced

over, as did everyone present. Tristan Holt was standing in front of her, close as though they'd been having an intimate chat. While we all stared, she slapped him in the face with her open palm, nearly backhanding Philip Hazeltine in the process. He'd been standing to the left of her. "You get away from me!" She sounded half hysterical. Her American friend, Irving, came rushing up to her side and, since the whole room had suddenly gone quiet, he said, "This kid's had way too much to drink. He made a pass at Candy. Get him out of here."

Lochlan couldn't live the billionaire lifestyle without having security, and two burly-looking guys in black suits appeared like magic. Tristan raised his hands as though in surrender. "I'm going," he said and then turned tail and headed for the exit, closely followed by two shadows.

Well, that was disappointing. He'd seemed like a nice guy, too. Lochlan sent me a glance as though thinking about rescinding my standing invitation to invite anybody I wanted to his castle. I didn't really blame him.

There was a minute or so of awkwardness, and then, the way a pond's surface gets still again after a stone has been thrown into it, the party was soon rolling along as though Tristan's bad behavior had never taken place.

I knew the schedule, and at the pre-appointed hour of nine o'clock, Giles Montague, Bartholomew Branson's editor, looking very dashing in a dark suit, stepped up to the raised stage that had been erected in the room, took the microphone and asked for everyone's attention. The chamber orchestra stopped playing and we all turned, sipping our drinks and waiting for the speech. He began by thanking everyone for coming. "Like all of you, I was thrilled to read every new Branson novel. I was especially privileged to be one of the first readers." He talked about *A Killer in His Sights* and how much he'd enjoyed working with Bartholomew Branson. I had no idea whether his words were sincere or not, but I knew how much the author upstairs would value them.

Giles spoke for about ten minutes, reminiscing about his years working with Bartholomew. He had a humorous anecdote to share about a confusing incident with a cab and getting lost while he and the author were attending the Frankfurt book fair. We all laughed dutifully. Once more, he thanked everyone for coming. There was polite applause, and then just as people were about to go back to their interrupted conversations and the orchestra was about to strike up again, Candace Branson walked up onto the stage.

This wasn't on any schedule I'd seen, and by the look on Giles Montague's face, he was a bit shocked too when she held out her hand for the microphone. Being a polite Englishman, what could he do? He passed it to her.

I didn't like the look of this.

She took his place and said into the microphone, "I'm sure I know most of you, but for those of you who don't know me, my name is Candace Branson. That's right, Branson. I had the honor to be Bartholomew Branson's wife and his literary partner for all the years of our marriage." She stopped to dab the corner of her eye with a fingertip.

"As Giles said, it's terribly tragic that we lost this major literary talent, but I also lost my heart. I lost my Barty."

I hoped she would get on with it, because her beloved Barty would not be very pleased to have her take the limelight away from his launch.

She said, "But I have a surprise for all of you. Something I know will bring some light into the sadness of losing him."

I hadn't noticed that she'd brought her handbag up with her until she reached into it and pulled out a thick sheaf of pages with a rubber band around the middle. Oh, I was getting a bad feeling about this. Instinctively, I cast a nervous glance around and caught Lochlan already moving toward the stairs that led to where Bartholomew was watching his party on closed-circuit TV.

She waved the thick pile of pages in the air. "I am thrilled to announce that when I was going through my beloved, and sadly departed, husband's things, I discovered a previously unpublished manuscript."

CHAPTER 8

There was a stunned silence around the room, and then Giles turned to her and said, "I beg your pardon?" He didn't sound exactly happy with her news. I supposed he didn't like being blindsided. "Did you say you were in possession of an unpublished manuscript by Bartholomew Branson?"

"That's right," she said, looking smug. She waved it under his nose. "It's called *All Fall Down.*"

People began to move towards her, and then from above came a terrible sound. It sounded like growling and snapping of teeth. Lochlan was running towards the stairs. I ran too.

"What is that?" Candace asked, nervously looking up.

Lochlan, halfway up the stairs, turned back and said, "Don't worry. It's just my dog. Carry on, I'll take care of it."

By the time we'd gotten to the top of the stairs, Bartholomew was being held back by Thomas Blood, a strapping vampire who'd been a colorful scoundrel in the sixteen hundreds, and three other strong vampires, and he nearly broke away from them. Lochlan Balfour, however, was an alpha vampire if there was such a thing. He stood over the author and said, coldly, "Go back inside."

Bartholomew Branson's face was contorted with fury. His teeth bared. Being human, I instinctively took a step back. He had bloodlust in his eyes.

It took all of them, including Lochlan, to force Bartholomew back into the room where he'd been watching the launch party. Lochlan led the way into a deeper part of the castle where the aggrieved author could yell and scream all he liked and not be heard outside of the thick walls of the turret. I knew this because this was where they kept Thomas Blood when he was being difficult.

Bartholomew paced back and forth. "I'll kill her."

"Am I correct in assuming there was no unpublished manuscript?" I said.

"Of course not. Everything I've ever written has been published."

"Where did she get that manuscript, then?"

"I'm too angry to think."

Oscar Wilde strolled in, looking happier than he had all day. "I can tell you how she did it."

We all turned to look at him.

"She listened to the screechings of a family of baboons and wrote it down."

Bartholomew was so full of fury, he looked happy to have somebody to fight with, and he launched himself at Oscar Wilde. Luckily, four strong vamps pulled him off before he could do any damage.

"So you'll have another book published posthumously," I said, trying to put a good face on things.

"But I didn't write that book. That harridan must have hired someone."

I stared at him. "Like a ghostwriter."

"That must be it."

"Let's hope it's a ghost with some semblance of literary talent," Oscar chimed in.

We all ignored him. Even Bartholomew. "That woman ruined my life. Now she's ruining my afterlife. This is a disaster. I have a posthumous manuscript of my own I'm working on," he said. No wonder he was angry. How many undiscovered manuscripts could one dead author have?

I wasn't a big drinker, but Lochlan Balfour's Irish whiskey was indeed smooth, and after the shock of discovering there was yet another posthumous manuscript, I really needed a drink.

"What are we going to do?" I asked.

Bartholomew was so enraged, he couldn't even string words together coherently. He just made sounds that I imagined an angry, rabid dog might make. There was a lot of snapping of teeth and foaming at the mouth.

Lochlan managed to remain cool. "We will, of course, attempt to stop the publication of a novel that you clearly didn't write."

I was a bit confused still. "Why would she do it? You're absolutely sure you didn't have an old manuscript lying around somewhere?"

"Of course not. It's like saying to a mother, 'Are you sure you didn't have another child that you forgot about?' An author doesn't forget his literary creations."

I glared at Oscar, and he shut his mouth again.

"But what's in it for her?" I asked. Candace did not strike

me as a woman whose main interest was her ex-husband's literary fame.

"Money, of course," he snapped.

"Bartholomew, is it possible you never changed your will after you got divorced?"

He looked sulky and uncomfortable. "I was in the prime of my life. I thought I had years to go before the grim reaper snatched me away."

"But she's your ex-wife."

"She's also my next of kin. There is no one else. Parents are dead, no brothers and sisters, never had any children."

"So if she comes out with a posthumous Branson novel, she'll make a killing."

"She'll make a killing on this one too."

I was curious about something. "Then why are you putting so much effort into writing a new book? You'll only be giving your ex-wife more money."

He looked sheepish. "I don't write just for the money. I love to write, Quinn. I don't want to disappoint my fans."

I didn't even turn my head this time. I just held up a single finger in Oscar Wilde's direction.

Lochlan said, "I've got to go back downstairs, as I'm hosting this gala. Quinn, you'd better come too." He stared at Bartholomew. "You will stay here. We will work on this problem together, do you understand?"

"Yes."

We went back downstairs to find that Candace was the center of an excited group. Philip Hazeltine and Giles Montague were in a corner, talking softly. No doubt it was being in an old castle that made me fanciful, but they reminded me of disloyal courtiers plotting to overthrow a king.

Still, the atmosphere was more party than political coup. Sean's food was a big hit, as was Lochlan's whiskey. However, my pleasure in the evening had been ruined. I'd become grudgingly fond of Bartholomew, and I didn't like the way this evening had turned from triumph to finding out his conniving widow was using his death to make a buck.

I stayed until the last guest left, then followed Lochlan back upstairs. I was worried about Bartholomew.

By this time, it was after midnight. The author had calmed down, but he still appeared agitated. "Guys, I need to get out and get some air."

We all looked at him sharply. He threw his hands up. "What? I'm not going to do anything. I just need to clear my head. It's been a shock."

Lochlan said, "Francis and Allan, go with him."

"What? Now you're going to treat me like you treat Thomas Blood? What do you think I'm going to do, try to steal the Crown Jewels?"

"No. I think you might go and see your ex-wife. And that would be disastrous."

"Well, I'm not. I promise."

"Nevertheless, you won't leave this castle alone."

"I don't appreciate the lack of trust," Bartholomew said with outraged dignity. Lochlan didn't budge, so reluctantly, he accepted the escort.

I looked around. They were all getting ready to go out somewhere. When the living population was sleeping was when the vampires could roam freely. I was very much in the way. "Well, I guess I'd better go home."

"I'll escort you, Quinn," Lochlan said.

I appreciated his old-fashioned protective manners, but I was an independent woman. "That's okay. I'm perfectly capable of getting home by myself."

"I insist. You never know what creatures are lurking out there after midnight."

There was a humorous glint in his eye. Sometimes I had to remind myself that he came from a time when chivalry was a real thing.

As we walked out of the castle, I said, "Did you ever joust?"

He laughed. "Now you're taking me back to my boyhood."

"You'll have to tell me all about it."

I thought I could grow to love history if I saw it through the eyes of someone who'd lived it.

As we walked back downstairs and through the great gallery, Sean was about to leave. "Great job," I told the pub owner and caterer. "The food was fabulous."

"I think everyone had a good time," he replied. Modest. I liked that.

"Quinn's right. You did an excellent job," Lochlan said. "Thank you."

"No worries. Oh, I found a pair of glasses when I was cleaning up." He waved a pair of gold-rimmed glasses in the air.

"Those belong to Giles Montague," I said, recognizing them immediately. "He's staying at O'Donnell House, so I can take them to him if you like."

"You're not going to the bed and breakfast at midnight, are you?"

"No. I'll go in the morning. I'm sure if Giles hasn't missed them by now, he won't need them before the morning. I'll email Karen anyway to let her know I've got them."

I tucked the glasses into my bag, and we followed Sean out of the castle.

Lochlan put my bike in the back of his Landrover and drove me home. He unloaded my bike when we got to my cottage, insisted on helping me secure it and very properly escorted me to my door and then said goodnight. It was so weird, almost like a date, and I had this kind of strange feeling of disquiet coursing through my veins. On impulse, I said, "Do you want to come in?" I didn't have anything particularly racy in mind. I just thought we could both wind down from the evening. Maybe talk about how we were going to stop Candace from cashing in on her dead ex-husband's fame.

He hesitated and then said, "I would, but I promised my printer friend a game of chess. And he did do us a favor."

I felt suddenly embarrassed. "No. Of course. Have a good night. I hope you win."

I let myself into the house, and the sense of unease only grew stronger. Then I heard a sound I was beginning to know all too well. The opening music for a certain television show. I stomped up the stairs. "Biddy? What are you doing here?"

The old witch wasn't just in my house; she was lying on my bed, her horrible, mangy familiar beside her. They both turned beady, unpleasant eyes on me. "You've let that girl fill my house with strangers. What do you expect? I have to go somewhere."

Her old leather bag looked particularly bulky, and the antique carriage clock that had been on top of my mantelpiece in the bedroom was missing. "Give me back my clock."

She started to argue with me, pretending she didn't have it, and I just stood there and glared at her until reluctantly she pulled it out.

"Fine. But for what I could sell this timepiece for, I could have bought fifty hectares of the finest land and three hundred head of sheep to graze it."

"Now you can buy a clock. And you'd be welcome to buy your own and not steal mine." It wasn't even mine. The clock belonged to Lucinda, the witch who had had the shop before me.

Biddy turned back to the TV, which was blaring full blast. Maybe in the middle of the day or early evening I'd have been quite interested in the price of a watercolor by an obscure British painter, but it was after midnight, and I was tired. "Biddy, I need to go to bed now."

She heaved a huge sigh as though this was a terrible imposition and shuffled about two inches over on the bed. As she moved, the scent of decay and earth emanated from her like a rank perfume.

I put my hands on my hips and glared at her. "You can't stay here."

"Well, where would you have me go?"

"You'll be going back to witch jail if you're not careful. You know that if Pendress Kennedy ever finds out that you're here, she'll send you back."

She snorted. "Let her try."

I had no idea which of them was the more powerful, and I really didn't want to be part of a showdown. For now, I was really hoping we could all just try to get along. But Biddy was not an easy person to get along with.

Instead of leaving, she turned the volume up even higher.

This was too much. "Are you going deaf?"

"I've been ever so hard of hearing since I was dug up," she admitted. She dug a bony finger into her ear and flung out a lump of dirt. Onto my bedspread. Lovely.

Then she turned her attention back to *Antiques Roadshow*.

An even worse smell curdled the air. Either Biddy or her familiar had farted.

I'm normally a peaceable witch, but I'd had a long night, led up to by several very long days, and I was not going to put up with this.

I drew on my powers and pointed to the TV.

"Goddesses of the north, south, east, and west, I call
on thee.
When this witch wants to watch TV.
Anything but *Antiques Roadshow* will she see.
So I will, so mote it be."

The station immediately flipped to BBC news. "Ha," I said, "take that."

Biddy mumbled something under her breath. I assumed she was grumbling because she'd have to find something else to do now that I'd taken away her favorite show. But, to my horror, the station flipped back again.

"Oh, no," I cried. "What did you do?"

"I reversed your spell, you foolish witch."

I cried out with rage and frustration. I grabbed the remote and punched buttons, but there was nothing to be seen but the *Antiques Roadshow*. I was so mad, I stomped over to the wall and yanked the power cord out of the wall.

I could see she was about to magic the TV back on when I

pointed my finger at her. "I'm warning you. You turn that TV on one more time, and I'm calling Pendress Kennedy."

I was like a kid threatening to tell on her to Mom. But, surprisingly, it worked. Biddy O'Donnell wasn't afraid of many things, but I had a sneaking suspicion she was afraid of Pendress Kennedy. I didn't blame her. So was I.

With a sniff, she said, "Never have been treated so poorly by my own kin."

And right back at you.

She got up, and Pyewacket rose too, arching her back and hissing at me. Since Pyewacket's neck had never been quite right since she was hanged, her head wobbled to the side and got stuck there. The two of them left, and I heaved a sigh of relief. Then I immediately changed the sheets on my bed.

I tried the TV, but the old hag had out-spelled me. No matter what I tried, the only thing that would play on my set was *Antiques Roadshow.*

I only wished I could sell one extremely old witch.

CHAPTER 9

 n spite of the drama and stress, I slept surprisingly well. I bet that when I did the accounting for the month, I'd be pleasantly surprised.

I got up, brewed coffee, and Cerridwen, who I hadn't seen all night, stuck her head through the cat door and sniffed before entering the premises.

"It's all right. They're gone," I told her. Only then did she come inside the kitchen. I fed her and apologized for my horrible ancestor. A bowl of food did much to recover Cerridwen's goodwill. I thought I'd better return Giles Montague's glasses before he set off back to London.

Before I left my cottage, I sprinkled salt across both entrances to the house and cast the whole house under a protection spell. Maybe Biddy could cross my threshold anyway, but I wanted to remind her she wasn't welcome to come and go whenever she pleased.

When I got to O'Donnell House, Karen looked delighted to see me. "Come in," she said. "They've been talking nonstop about the gala."

I stepped in, and sure enough I heard the sound of laughter and camaraderie. It was nice.

"Too bad you couldn't come."

"I know. I wanted to, but I needed to get the food prepared for the breakfasts this morning." She dropped her voice. "These early reviews will be so important, you see. I really pulled out all the stops."

I walked into the dining room, pretty sure I'd be welcome, and sure enough Giles rose to his feet. Philip then followed suit. Irving gave me a wave, and Chloe nodded.

"Quinn," Giles said. "It's lovely to see you. This saves us coming to the shop to bid you goodbye properly. Please, sit down and join us. Can I pour you some coffee?"

Since this wasn't his house, but Karen's, I glanced up at our hostess. She said, "Yes. Do sit down and have some coffee."

"Sure, if it's no trouble." I wanted to hear what they had to say about last night, too. Especially as it concerned a certain manuscript. From the jovial atmosphere, it seemed they'd decided to greet Candace's bombshell as good news.

"And have some breakfast," Karen added. "I've the full Irish breakfast, eggs benedict, kippers, or Irish oatmeal, fruit and yogurt—"

"Stop. If you're absolutely sure, I'll have the full Irish breakfast." I hardly ever indulged in the full Irish breakfast, and it was a treat well worth having. Especially when somebody else cooked it.

She winked at me. "I'll be back in a jiff."

I returned Giles's glasses to him, and he thanked me profusely.

Everyone was there but Candace. I remarked on this, and

Irving made a face. "I think our Candy tucked into the Irish whiskey a little too deeply last night. She's probably sleeping it off."

Karen walked in then, carrying a heavy tray laden with plates of food and sending out the most mouthwatering smells of bacon, coffee, and sausages.

She placed big breakfasts in front of everyone but Chloe, who had chosen the healthy fresh fruit and yogurt option.

We all tucked in to our breakfasts, then Giles said, "I'd have missed my glasses last night if I hadn't been so knackered I went straight to bed. I was going to ask Candace for a look at that new manuscript she's discovered."

The British agent said, "Don't worry, old chap. I'll make sure you get it as soon as I've had a good look at it." His choice of words was interesting. Not that he'd read it, but that he'd have a good look at it. Made me wonder whether he suspected Bartholomew hadn't written this miraculously discovered work.

Irving rubbed his nose and said, "Yeah, about that. I think Candy's going in a different direction." He pushed his fork into a fat mushroom. "She's asked me to be her agent."

Philip Hazeltine threw his napkin on the table and rose so quickly, his chair jerked backwards. "I knew it. I suspected you were up to something, you swine."

Giles looked from Chloe to me. "Gentlemen, please."

Philip said, "Ha. He's no gentleman. He's a cad and a bounder."

Irving spread his hands, a smug smile spreading over his face. "Just other words for a literary agent."

Karen came in carrying a fresh plate of toast and glanced around. It must have been a shock to her to walk into the kitchen leaving behind a convivial atmosphere and walk back five minutes later to a tense standoff.

She didn't say anything, just slipped the toast on the table.

Giles, once more the peacemaker, said, "Gentlemen, please. Let's sit down and discuss this like civilized people. At least, let's wait for Candace to appear. She can tell us her plans herself."

Philip looked as though he was ready to storm out but reluctantly picked up his napkin and sat down again. I was very pleased to see this, as I really wanted to enjoy my full Irish.

I tucked into my fried eggs and bacon, beans, mushroom, and sausage. Even the toast was delicious. And what was it about Irish butter? It was just so creamy.

Philip stabbed a triangle of toast into a fried egg the way he'd have thrust a dueling saber into Irving's plump belly.

"I have a contract with Bartholomew Branson," he said.

Irving cut into his fat sausage. "But contracts expire when the person who signed them dies."

I had no idea if this was true but suspected it was.

I thought Philip knew it too. He glared from Irving to Giles. "Can't you do something?"

Giles shrugged his thin shoulders. "I'm only the editor."

Irving said, around another bite of sausage, "Yeah, about that. We're going to be shopping the new manuscript. See if we can get a better deal."

Suddenly, Giles didn't look so urbane and so much like a peacemaker. He looked coldly furious. "I have edited every Branson novel. I discovered him when he was nobody. Why, he'd turn in his grave if he knew how you were treating his trusted team. We'll see about that."

Irving finished his breakfast in about half the time the rest of us took and mopped the last of the egg yolk and grease off his plate. He said, "Hate to eat and run, folks, but Candy and I need to get on the road."

He reached over for the silver carafe in the center of the table and poured coffee into a clean mug. "I'll take her up some coffee. I'm sure she'll tell you all her plans when she comes down."

No one stopped him from leaving. Chloe and Giles glanced at each other, but almost by silent, unspoken agreement, I could tell they didn't want to talk anymore in front of me. Which was fine by me.

Irving whistled as he walked up the stairs, which I thought was pretty crass. We all knew he'd won. He didn't need to rub it in.

I heard his heavy footsteps go up the stairs. Giles pulled his urbanity back around him like a cardigan and complimented me on the splendid launch. I'd barely replied when weirdly, I heard Irving's heavy footsteps thudding back down the stairs as though he were running. He burst into the dining room. He was bright red in the face and sweating.

I wondered if he might be having a heart attack. His mouth opened and shut as he stared around the room. All of us stopped eating and stared back.

"Which of you did it?" he shouted.

"Did what?" I asked.

"Which of you killed Candace?"

CHAPTER 10

here was a moment of stunned silence, and then Giles said, in a voice more shocking because it was so quiet, "Did you say Candace Branson is dead?"

"Not just dead. Murdered." He was standing there, big and red-faced and sweating as though he'd got stuck.

I swallowed a bite of toast, and it seemed to jam in my throat. I jumped to my feet, recalling hearing Irving's feet stomp along the upstairs corridor and stomp back again. He hadn't been gone very long. "Are you sure? Maybe the Irish whiskey really knocked her out."

He just shook his head.

I hadn't particularly liked Candace Branson, but I also wasn't prepared to take Irving's word for it that she was dead. Not if there was any chance at all that she might still be alive. I had to edge my way around Irving to get through the doorway, and then I ran lightly up the stairs. I felt as though I were hitting a patch of cold fog as I got upstairs. I headed for the front bedroom and found that Irving had been right.

She was definitely dead. I felt the darkness almost

pushing back as I ran into the room. To make matters worse, Biddy was there, gazing down at the corpse with cool detachment.

"She's been strangled," Biddy said to me. I could see she was right. The dead woman lay across the bed. She was on her back, her eyes wide and her face discolored. Livid bruises marked her neck. I glanced up at Biddy.

"Did you see who did it?"

"No, love. I was watching the telly."

Of course, she had been.

"What about last night? Did you see her at all?" I knew that Biddy wasn't one to respect closed doors. Especially as she considered this was her own house and I'd thrown her out of my cottage.

She shook her head.

"I came a few times, and once I even put the television on as a suggestion like. There were some very nice ceramics that I wouldn't have given a tuppence for, went for hundreds of quid, they did. But all she did was get in a huff and stomp over and turn off the television. She was too busy reading them pages."

I glanced sharply up at her. "What pages?"

Biddy opened her hands. "How would I know what pages? A stack of separate papers with writing on them. Like household receipts."

"Like a book manuscript?"

"I never had much time for reading, myself. Wouldn't know."

I glanced around, but there was no sign of the manuscript. "Did you see where she put it?"

But Biddy faded away and then disappeared as the sound

of running footsteps grew nearer. Karen and Giles and Philip looked as though they were going to come crashing into the room.

"Stop," I said before any of them crossed the threshold. "She's dead. There's nothing we can do for her. And Irving's right. She was murdered. We can't contaminate the crime scene any more than we already have."

I sounded like a bad actor in a cop show, but the truth was I'd had some recent experience with murder scenes. Irving lumbered up last, bringing up the rear.

"Has anyone called the police?"

Karen nodded. "Chloe called 999. Police are on their way."

I stepped back out of the room and, using my T-shirt to cover my hand, carefully shut the door. "No one else must go in there until the police arrive," I said.

It didn't look like anybody was in a rush to go inside Candace's room anyway, but I thought it was best to be sure.

I looked at them all. "Which of you has the manuscript?"

They all looked in various ways sick or pale or just shocked. Now every pair of eyes turned to me. In Karen's, I only saw curiosity, but the others were sharply inquisitive.

"What do you mean, who's got the manuscript?" Irving asked me. "Candy had it. She wanted to finish reading it last night before she passed it on to me."

I shook my head. "The manuscript is gone."

Giles was the only one who didn't shout. He said, "Are you certain, Quinn?"

"Not positively certain. But her reading glasses were beside her on the bed as though she'd been interrupted. The manuscript is not on the bed, it's not on the side table, and it's not on the dressing table. It's also not on the floor. So unless she's put it away somewhere, it's gone."

Karen Tate said, "If I'm reading in bed, I put my book away first and then take off my reading glasses. She could have tucked it away in a bag or even her suitcase as she was leaving this morning."

That was a good point. The police would soon know if the manuscript was in her things, but I had a suspicion that whoever had killed her had wanted those pages.

Irving spluttered, "It must be there." He took a step forward and, even though he was a lot bigger than I, I stayed where I was in front of that door. He recollected himself and said, "It must be in there. It must."

I wasn't so sure. "When the police get here, they'll search the room thoroughly, and then we'll know for sure."

He wiped the sweat off his forehead with the back of his wrist. "I can't get over it. Candy? She was my whole life. We had such plans."

"Your whole life? I thought you were her agent."

"We were keeping it on the down-low, but I was a lot more than her agent. We were going to get married."

"Well, somebody decided to stop her before she could complete those plans."

We stood there crowded in the hallway for another minute, and then Giles said, "I think I'll just go to my room and..." He petered out. I got the feeling he didn't know what to do with himself any more than the rest of us did.

Perhaps he just wanted to privately mourn or to brush his teeth or something. But Irving said in a loud voice, "Oh no. I bet you stole that manuscript, you slimy, British pencil pusher. I'm not letting you out of my sight. You'll try to hide it, maybe burn it. I wouldn't trust you further than I could throw you."

Giles drew himself up to his full height. "Don't be impertinent. I wish she'd given me that book for safekeeping. How I wish it. But she didn't."

Irving's shock was wearing off, being replaced by an unpleasant belligerence. "Well, somebody's got it. And none of you are getting out of my sight until the cops get here."

There was some grumbling, but he was right, and we all knew it. And if somebody here had the manuscript, he, or she, was likely Candace Branson's murderer.

Karen, who was really impressing me as a bed and breakfast hostess, took charge. "Why don't you all come back downstairs. I'll put the fire on in the front room and bring some more coffee. You can all wait there until the police want to talk to you."

"After you," Giles said to Irving with exaggerated politeness. The three men walked ahead of us, and Karen waited until they'd started down the stairs before turning back to me. "What rotten luck. I mean, I'm sorry for that woman, naturally, but is this house cursed? That's the third death in that room this year."

She didn't even know about Biddy. I shook my head. "I don't think so. Bad luck, more like. Try not to worry."

She rubbed her temple as though she was getting a headache. "I've put everything into this place, Quinn. My inheritance, all my savings. I borrowed money. If word gets out one of my first house guests was murdered, what will that do to my business?"

That was an unanswerable question, and I didn't even try. I put a hand on her arm. "You didn't murder that woman.

Someone else did. The police will figure out who did it and we'll move on. Besides, the way I look at it, even if word gets out about what really happened here, it will probably only bring in more Bartholomew Branson fans."

She made a face. "That wasn't exactly how I'd planned to increase my business."

"Well, beggars can't be choosers and all that," I said. "You go on down now. I'll stay here until the Gardai arrive. I don't trust any of them downstairs."

We could both hear sirens now. I wouldn't have long to wait.

Karen went downstairs, and soon I heard voices and then people coming up the stairs. Seeing the paramedics pause at the top, I called out, "She's in here."

They ran forward, and I stayed outside, obviously, as they went in. They left the door open, but they could very quickly see there was no hope for the woman lying on the bed. Still, they examined her.

The house began to fill very quickly after that.

Two detectives I'd come to know arrived when I was still upstairs. Detective Inspector Walsh and Sergeant Kelly.

"Quinn Callahan," the older detective said. "Fancy seeing you here."

"Good morning, Detective." DI Walsh looked like a boxer who'd been knocked out more often than he'd won. His nose had clearly been broken more than once, and he had a tough-guy body and attitude.

"What happened here?"

I shook my head. "I really don't know."

"This is a bed and breakfast. Don't you live here in town?"

Why did the most innocent actions always seem imbued with criminal intent when describing them to a police officer? I felt flustered, and I'm certain it showed. "I do. I live in a cottage on the edge of town. But one of the gentlemen staying here left his glasses behind last night at the gala launch of Bartholomew Branson's posthumous thriller novel." I was giving way too many details. I needed to rein it in. "I was worried that he might leave town without realizing they were missing, and so I brought the glasses over here this morning. And then, since I caught them at breakfast, they invited me to join them."

"I see." He kept staring at me in a way I found extremely uncomfortable. As though he knew there were questions he wanted to ask me but he couldn't quite put his finger on them. I understood completely how he felt. My brain was brimming with questions too. And I wasn't sure which were the right ones to ask.

Finally, he went with, "Did you know the victim?"

"Yes." I explained that she was the former wife of the sadly deceased Bartholomew Branson and that she'd come to Ballydehag for the launch of his posthumous novel.

"So they were on good terms then?" Sergeant Kelly asked me.

Now that was a sticky one. I couldn't tell him that I knew they weren't on good terms because the vampire had told me so. On the other hand, I couldn't pretend they'd been a happily divorced couple. I shrugged. "Candace Branson insisted that she and her ex-husband were on very good terms. However, they must have gotten divorced for a reason. And I didn't get the feeling that his editor and agent believed they'd been quite so happy. Or quite so amicable."

"That's interesting. So she came all the way to Ireland for the launch of her dead husband's book?"

"That's right."

"After they'd been divorced for how long?"

"I really don't know."

"Well, I suppose we can't look to the husband, which is the usual place we begin our inquiries in a place like this."

"Why not?" the sergeant asked.

"Because he's dead," I reminded him.

"In actual fact, we don't know that."

I stared at him with my jaw dropping. Did the sergeant believe in vampires? You could never tell.

But DI Walsh merely nodded thoughtfully. "I take your point, Kelly. Bartholomew Branson went missing from a cruise ship off the coast of Ireland and was never seen again. We've been assuming he was drowned, but no body was ever discovered."

"But where else could he be?" I asked. Hoping very much that they never discovered he was within five miles. And while not exactly alive, he was not exactly dead either.

"You didn't discover the body, did you?" DI Walsh asked me.

I was happy to tell him no. Irving Schultz had that distinction. Then I had to admit that I had entered the dead woman's room.

"Why?"

"I wasn't certain Irving was right. He was upstairs and back so fast. I hated to think she might need medical attention but didn't get it because we all took Irving's word for it that she was dead." I squeezed my eyes shut, wishing I had believed the man and hadn't had to see poor Candace like that. "So I went into her room. She'd been strangled and was very obviously dead."

"All right, you can go now," DI Walsh said.

I was glad to get away from death. Happy to get out of this house and back to my cottage. However, when I got to the bottom of the stairs, Karen was just coming in from the kitchen with a tray of coffee.

"Quinn, please don't leave me. The lounge is like, I don't know what, an animal cage. Only they've put the wrong animals together. Giles is smooth and cool like a particularly deadly snake. Irving reminds me of a wild boar. He's snuffling the ground and dying to gore somebody to death, but he doesn't know who. Chloe is like a fox with small, sharp teeth, but I wouldn't want to turn my back on her. While Philip is like a lion. Sitting all proud and stately, but his teeth are sharp and his claws are ready to rip."

"You are not selling me on spending time with them," I told her. I really wanted to go home, but the desperate look on her face filled me with sympathy. "That coffee better be fresh."

She grinned at me. "Quinn, I don't know what I'd do without you. If it's not fresh enough, I'll go and brew you a fresh pot."

I held the door to the lounge room open for her, and as I followed her in, I understood exactly what she meant. I'd heard the expression you could cut the atmosphere with a knife before, but for this atmosphere? You'd pretty much need a chainsaw. None of the three men in the room were looking at each other, but that somehow made it worse. Irving was glaring into the fire that was burning and crackling away, oblivious. Philip had picked up a book off the shelves and was perusing it. Since all the books in this lounge had come from my shop, I knew perfectly well that they were on that shelf for their beautiful covers and not for the contents. Dredging my memory, I suspected he was reading the sermons of Charles Haddon Spurgeon. Besides, the pages had yellowed and foxed and the print was tiny. I didn't think he was reading it at all; he was just keeping himself occupied.

Giles was staring out the window, probably wishing, like I did, that he was on the other side of it, and Chloe was typing away on her laptop.

The tray rattled when Karen placed it on the coffee table, and she looked at me, opening her eyes wide in appeal. The universal distress signal for, "Do something."

Okay. I asked, "Who wants coffee?" in a bright voice that sounded false to my ears.

"I couldn't," Giles said without even turning his gaze my way.

"Not for me," Philip said.

"Coffee?" Chloe said, looking up. "Lovely. I take it black." As though this was a normal morning and time for her regular coffee break. She was a cool customer, that one.

"Yeah, I'll take some," Irving said, turning from his contemplation of the fire. "Cream and sugar."

Pouring two cups of coffee and doctoring one with milk and sugar at least gave me something to do for a minute or so. Then I poured myself a cup.

The strained silence descended once more. I tried to think of a subject of conversation that was both neutral and dull enough that we could bat it around until the police had finished with us.

Naturally, everything I came up with immediately raised

disaster flares in my head. Branson's new book? Oh no. Their travel plans for back home? Oh no. This previously undiscovered work by the author?

Oh. No.

I put my coffee cup down so hard, the coffee geysered and dribbled over the edge. Bartholomew Branson's undiscovered manuscript. I knew it wasn't a Branson. Candace Branson knew it wasn't authentic. I strongly suspected Irving knew, but the one who had the biggest problem with Candace's attempt to make money off her dead ex-husband was the dead ex-husband himself.

Bartholomew Branson. I'd been there when he'd insisted on going out. He'd promised he'd stay away from his ex, but the promise of a furious vampire was probably not on the same level as a promise made by, say, Charles Haddon Spurgeon, Baptist minister and prolific sermon writer.

"Did Candace have any visitors last night?" I asked. The atmosphere was strained anyway. What difference did it make if I asked searching questions about the murder investigation?

At least that had the effect of getting everybody's attention.

Giles turned back from the window. "I heard voices in her bedroom. It's next to mine. But I assumed it was one of us." And then he glared at Irving, who reddened under the supercilious gaze.

"Don't look at me. I was in my own room. Candace was busy going over that book."

Philip said, "I certainly didn't go into her room last night."

"Nor I," Chloe said.

"No. Couldn't have been you, Chloe. I'm almost certain it was a man and woman I heard."

Oh, great. I could imagine Bartholomew Branson barging his way in here without thinking through the consequences. Suppose he'd gone to visit his ex-wife? Once she knew he was undead, maybe he couldn't trust her to keep his secret. Maybe he decided to stop her mouth permanently.

CHAPTER 11

*I*t made me sad to think of Bartholomew as a murderer. To think I'd helped organize the launch that led to Candace's death.

Philip said, "I wonder if it was that young fellow who looked like a student. He and Candace had quite an intense conversation at the launch party at the castle."

Irving laughed. "Intense conversation? She slapped his face."

I didn't want to think of Tristan Holt as a murderer any more than I wanted it to be Bartholomew. "Did any of you see that guy near here?"

They glanced among themselves and shook their heads.

Irving continued, "But Candy was real upset. Said he was coming on to her."

As a forty-five-year-old woman, I was the last person to scoff at a young man being smitten with an older woman, but I doubted Tristan Holt had had romance in mind when he spoke to Candace Branson.

I turned to Giles. "You heard Candace speaking with

someone through the walls of a pretty solidly built building. Any chance you recognized the voice?"

He rocked back and forth on his heels as though trying to take himself back. "No. But now I think of it, I believe it was American and young. Yes, I believe so."

How convenient to cast suspicion on someone who wasn't staying at O'Donnell House. Had Giles really heard a young American in Candace's room, or was he trying to cast suspicion away from himself?

Even if I assumed he was telling the truth, it wasn't much to go on. However, if that manuscript was missing, someone had taken it. Unfortunately, the prime suspect in my mind had to be Bartholomew. But if that young guy had come here to continue his discussion with Candace, he was a possible suspect too.

I wanted to ask more probing questions, but I was startled when the television sprang to life.

We all turned to stare at the screen. The familiar music from the *Antiques Roadshow* played, and then Fiona Bruce welcomed us to yet another fabulous British mansion loaded with history. The grounds were packed with antique lovers, some with their dogs and kids, some eating ice cream, and loads standing in line with bulging bags and carefully clutched boxes.

"Most odd the way that's the only television program that ever seems to play in this bed and breakfast," Giles said. But I noticed that he came away from the window and sat on the couch, where he had a good view of the television.

Philip put down the book he wasn't reading and sat on the opposite side of the couch.

Even Irving drifted away from his contemplation of the

fire and stood with his back against the wall. Chloe glanced up from her laptop, then went back to what she was doing.

No one seemed to notice that the remote was still sitting on top of the TV. And, presumably, no one but me was bothered by the scent of earth and decay.

Karen came in looking flustered. In a low voice, she said to me, "That music is doing my head in. How is it possible that televisions all over this building turn on spontaneously and they are always playing the same television show?"

I could have told her. But didn't. "I wouldn't worry about it," I said in a voice as low as hers had been. "Look at them. It's caught their attention. I no longer worry that they're going to kill each other, unless they bore each other with stories of how their great-grandfather had one of those Toby jugs, and if only they'd known it would be worth so much they'd have kept it all these years."

Her strained look vanished in a wry chuckle. "I do know what you mean. Perhaps I'll call it a mixed blessing."

And for now, it certainly was. Although why Biddy O'Donnell had chosen to put this television on was more than I could figure out. Maybe she was worried that if she did it upstairs, the police would investigate. Down here, where there was already noise and goings-on, perhaps she thought she'd get away with turning on her favorite show. And, looking at the three rapt faces currently finding out the provenance of a blue china plate with a maharaja's castle painted on it, she was right. For once in her unpleasant life, she'd done a good deed.

Since they were all happily, and quietly, engaged in the program, I motioned with my head for Karen and I to go outside into the corridor. We did, and she shut the door gently behind her.

I asked, keeping my voice low so the police didn't hear, "Did Candace Branson have a visitor last night?"

She shrugged. "The police already asked me that. But I don't know. I was so tired from the day, and knew I'd be up dreadfully early this morning to cook breakfast, that I went to bed early, long before my guests returned home."

That was unfortunate. "So you didn't hear anything?"

She looked uncomfortable. "The truth was, I got very interested in some of the earliest Waterford crystal. Remarkable the way they could make crystal three hundred years ago. And what some of that stuff is worth."

I didn't have to ask what television program she'd been watching. I strongly suspected she hadn't been alone. She'd had a witch of a roommate.

"But..." Her gaze shifted down the hall to the front door. "Now you mention it, I woke around one in the morning, it was, and then got up to make sure the front door was locked. Quinn, I'm sure I saw a pair of shoes I didn't recognize."

Nothing wonderful there. She did have bed and breakfast visitors. However, I said, "Yes?"

She squinted her eyes and kept staring down towards the front door. "They were trainers. I might not have noticed them particularly except they were rather dirty. Giles would certainly never wear that kind of shoe. Neither would Philip. Chloe only wears designer shoes. Irving, the American, might, but his feet are much larger. Besides, his cowboy boots were sitting on the same mat. It's rather American, isn't it, to take off one's shoes when entering another person's home?"

"Can be." I knew someone who had very dirty running shoes. Also, he was young and American.

I'd be very interested to know what Tristan Holt had been doing here last night. Was he visiting a woman who'd slapped his face in public?

If so, why?

The only problem was finding him.

I had a feeling that if the young man was still in town, I had to move fast. Once there was a police manhunt out for a young American, he'd be on the move, guilty or innocent. Whichever he was, I really wanted to talk to him.

I had no idea where to search for a twentysomething who had dirty sneakers, a grubby backpack, and didn't look like he had a lot of money. "Karen, is there a local hostel?"

"A hostel, Quinn? Why would you want one of those? If you've friends coming to visit, I'll give you mates' rates on staying here."

"Thanks," I said, genuinely touched. "But it's not for me."

"Well, there are hostels in Cork City. There might be something in Skibbereen, but I don't know. Never had occasion to stay in one."

"Thanks." I motioned to the closed door of the lounge. "They're all settled in front of the TV now. I really have to get back. I need to get The Blarney Tome put back together after the event last night."

I saw a flicker of dismay in her eyes, but she understood the challenges of running a small business. "Of course. Thank you so much for staying this morning. I don't know what I would have done without you."

"Anytime." I touched her shoulder. "Try not to worry. The police will find who did this, and your business will boom."

"I do hope so."

I didn't even bother saying goodbye to the literary types. I headed out, jumped in my car and started the engine. I drove down to the end of the block, wondering where I was going. I hadn't exactly lied to Karen. I did need to put the shop back to rights, but it didn't have to be this minute. The books would all still be there tomorrow, but a potential murderer might not.

I tried to think of who might help me track down Tristan Holt, and the only person who came to mind was Lochlan Balfour. While I hesitated to interrupt vampires in the day when they were getting their beauty sleep, Lochlan never seemed like he needed a great deal of rest. Besides, if he was sleeping, I'd go to the shop and get to work. So, sucking in a breath, I drove to Devil's Keep.

In truth, it looked more like Devil's Sleep. There wasn't a light on in the place, and I saw no signs of activity.

I got out of the car and stood at the entrance, wondering if I should turn around and go away again without bothering them. A voice said, "Are you coming in?" It was cool and slightly ironic. Lochlan.

I glanced around. I had no idea where he was hiding but answered him anyway. "I thought you might be sleeping."

The door in front of me magically opened, and I realized that he wasn't in the vicinity. He'd obviously spied me through some complicated security camera.

Well, at least I knew I wasn't waking him. I walked inside, and the thick, heavy, oak door made a definitive clunk behind me. I walked up the staircase into the big main room where we'd held the gala last night. The posters were still hanging, but all the food had been cleared away and the furniture put back.

While I was wondering where I might find my host, he appeared through a doorway at the back of the room. "Quinn." His tone was cordial but contained a note of question, as in, "Was I expecting you?"

I stepped closer. "The most terrible thing has happened." And I quickly told him about Candace's murder.

He glanced up, and I knew immediately he was looking towards wherever Bartholomew Branson might be tucked away. "Natural causes?" The question was hopeful rather than that he believed any such thing.

I shook my head. "She was strangled."

"What an unpleasant death."

He glanced up again. "Branson?" He'd come to the same conclusion as me, then. However, as though continuing on his train of thought, he said, "Not the way we vampires normally go about our business." Then he looked at me again. "You're absolutely certain she was strangled? It wasn't strangulation meant to cover up the real cause of death?"

Gross. "You mean bite marks?" I hadn't gotten that close to her, but I was pretty sure I'd have noticed if her blood had been drained. "No. I think she was just plain strangled."

Nothing in his expression changed, but I could tell he was relieved by my answer. "How can I help you?"

I liked that he got straight to the point. "You remember that young guy who was here last night? The one that Candace had thrown out?"

"Of course. That was the most exciting thing that happened all evening."

I was glad Bartholomew Branson, the thriller writer, wasn't present to hear those words.

"His name is Tristan Holt. Anyway, I think he might have visited her last night."

"They were certainly arguing. And she slapped him. You suspect he killed her?"

"I don't know. But he's what the cops would call a person of interest."

"Do you have any idea where he is?"

"No. That's what I was hoping you would help me with."

He came a step closer. "You want my help finding a missing person?"

"Well, that's the thing. I don't think he is missing. But he might still be in the area. I don't think he had a car. His shoes were muddy as though he'd been walking across rough ground. His backpack was grubby, and he looked like a backpacker."

He shook his head. "In any case, there won't be a bus out until this evening. We could check with Dylan's taxi and see if he got a ride somewhere."

"Is there a hostel?"

"It's thirty miles away. And they usually provide showers. Your young man looked, and smelled, as though he'd not bathed in several days." He turned to stare at one of Bartholomew Branson's covers. It featured a picture of the Kremlin and the silhouette of a man holding a pistol. "I wonder if he's been camping rough."

"Camping rough?"

"There's no hostel hereabouts. He wasn't staying in the bed and breakfast. He didn't look like he had any kin in the area. My guess is he was sleeping rough. That rucksack of his was big enough for a small tent or a tarp."

I nodded slowly. "That would explain the muddy shoes and the dirt underneath his fingernails. But he could be anywhere then, couldn't he?"

"Quinn. He's an American traveling in Ireland. He'd be drawn to the Wild Atlantic Way."

"Okay." The Wild Atlantic Way was one of the most picturesque drives in the world. But there was quite a lot of it. "Could you be more specific?"

He continued to stare at that book poster as though the young guy with the backpack might walk out of the Kremlin and surrender to the guy with the pistol. "I know a few likely spots."

He looked at what I was wearing and said, "Go home and put on some sturdier boots. Have you some good walking shoes?"

"Yeah. I've got my hiking boots from when I lived in Seattle."

"Those'll do. And some rugged clothes you don't mind getting mucky."

So not what I'd imagined doing this morning.

But then I hadn't imagined I'd be interrupted halfway through a full Irish breakfast because of a murder either.

It was turning out to be an unusual day.

CHAPTER 12

*T*hadn't worn hiking pants since before I left Seattle. In fact, now that I came to think of it, it was quite a long time before I left Seattle. However, I dug the hiking pants I'd so proudly bought at REI out of a box at the back of the cupboard, along with my hiking boots, and wondered how wild the Wild Atlantic Way really was. I'd driven it and admired spectacular views along the winding coastline, but I'd never attempted to track a possible murderer on foot. I hoped my old hiking gear was up to the task.

The first dent in the plan happened when my hiking pants got stuck halfway up my hips.

My irritable conviction that they'd somehow shrunk in transit died on the vine. I hopped my way to the full-length mirror in bra, panties, and the hiking trousers that were lodged on my thighs.

For some reason, I hopped in a circle just for the pleasure of getting a glimpse of my back view. It wasn't pretty.

How had I gained so much weight and not even noticed?

Cerridwen padded by on near-silent feet and paused to look at me. Cerridwen was not normally an unkind cat, but I definitely detected derision in her wide, green eyes.

"All right," I said. "I'm not getting enough exercise. Working in a bookstore isn't exactly aerobic." And the Irish food was so good. Also, much of it seemed to be based around starches. Irish stew, for instance, bursting with doughy dumplings. And what the Irish could do with a potato could make you weep.

Or overeat.

I couldn't have gained so much weight so fast without even noticing. Could I?

I'd always heard of middle-aged spread and suspected it was a lie put out by women who'd given up. Now, I begged to disagree. Middle age was spreading from my belly to my butt to my thighs, and it didn't look like it was finished yet.

Determined I was not going to let a pair of pants beat me, I began jumping up and down, yanking on the waistband every time I was in the air. I did manage to get the pants over my hips. Triumphant, I turned to look in the mirror, and the way they gaped and strained at the front, I knew I'd never get the zipper done up. And even if I did, I would not be able to breathe or speak.

Sweaty and bad-tempered, I gave up.

It was almost as much effort to get the trousers off again. I was panting and red in the face when I finally screwed the expensive, technical fabric hiking pants into a ball and threw them in the corner. Okay, I was having a tantrum.

Now what was I going to wear? Having grown up in the Pacific Northwest, I knew that jeans were the worst thing for hiking or even strenuous walking. The heavy cotton would attract and hold water, making the trouser both heavy and uncomfortably wet.

What else did I have that fit? Too cold for shorts, and I probably couldn't fit in them anyway. I finally settled on a pair of yoga pants that only fit me because of the stretchy waistband. I put a loose T-shirt over the top and the kind of zip-up hoodie girls wear to exercise class to keep their tiny bodies warm since they have no body fat to do it for them. In my case, I had no intention of taking this thing off. It would have to disguise all the lumpy, bumpy bits.

At least my hiking boots still fit. Though my big toes were pressing against the front of the boot in a way I didn't remember. Had my feet gotten fatter?

I found a ball cap that would at least protect me a little bit from the weather and threw a few essentials into a small day pack I used when I would go hiking for the day.

I had come to Ireland so certain I would be tramping the hills and admiring every wild corner of the Emerald Isle. Instead, all I ever seemed to see was the inside of the bookshop, the pub, and my cottage.

I was really going to have to make some time for exercise. Very soon.

I was going to have to start matching my fantasy self closer to the middle-aged woman I was rapidly becoming. Not that I minded being middle-aged. There was a lot that was good about knowing who I was and not being driven so much by my hormones.

Lochlan picked me up and drove. Dierdre had happily agreed to tend the bookshop, which gave me a day to track a murderer. Not my favorite pursuit on a day off, but I was the one who'd wanted to find this guy. The sun was shining, making the ocean sparkle. Even though this was a serious enterprise, I enjoyed the view as he drove, with the rugged coastline on one side and green fields dotted with sheep on the other. "Isn't there a lot of Wild Atlantic Way?" I finally asked.

"Mmm. Sixteen hundred miles of it. It's one of the longest coastal drives in the world."

"Sixteen hundred miles?" I turned in my seat to stare at his handsome profile. "But how will we find Tristan Holt?"

"I can't guarantee that we will. But if he's camping in the wild, which I suspect he is, it's the logical place to start."

"But there must be all sorts of thickets of trees and hidden coves. It'll be like a needle in a haystack."

He sent me a funny look. "Not quite. Needles in haystacks don't have beating hearts."

My own heart kicked up its beat at that. I turned to stare at him. "You can hear a human's beating heart?"

He raised his nose like a dog catching a particularly good scent. "It's more like we can smell them."

I was sort of horrified, but the practical side of me was relieved. "But can you differentiate one heartbeat from another?"

"Not really. You get to know certain patterns. Yours, I'd recognize anywhere."

He must really hear it thundering now. "You would?" I asked, and my voice came out a little higher than I'd meant it to.

He turned at me with barely suppressed humor in his eyes. "You're safe with me, you know."

Knowing he could hear my insanely rapid heartbeat

didn't make it any easier to slow it down. So I didn't even bother. "It's kind of creepy, you know, from where I sit."

"I can imagine it would be. But, as I said, you're in no danger from me."

My attention slipped away from Tristan Holt to the dead woman. "What about Candace Branson? If Bartholomew had been married to her, he must have known her heartbeat intimately."

"Likely he did. Though, to be fair, he wasn't a vampire when they were together."

"So you don't think he'd recognize her heartbeat?"

"No. I think he would. And if he didn't recognize her heartbeat, he could easily track her by her scent."

Oh man, this drive was just getting worse and worse. My underarms grew unpleasantly warm. I wanted to wipe my brow except it would look so obvious.

Change the subject, change the subject. "Can you think of a reason why Tristan Holt would kill Bartholomew Branson's ex-wife?"

Lochlan sent me a glance that was almost chiding. "Of course I can. And so can you."

How was he so smart? He hadn't had a long conversation with Tristan Holt, who had made me test his knowledge of the latest Bartholomew Branson novel and boasted about how well he knew the material.

I let out a breath. "I think he was Candace Branson's ghostwriter for *All Fall Down.*"

"Yes. I think so too."

It was so unfair. "How did you know that?"

"Process of elimination. He was far younger than most of

Branson's fans. He'd clearly come a long way knowing the author was dead. Based on the very public squabble, it was the author's widow he wished to see, and the visit didn't go well."

I wrinkled my nose. "Do you call it a widow when they've been divorced?"

He shook his head. "In my day, divorce was exceedingly rare. I have no idea."

"Anyway, go on."

"It was evident he didn't have much money, and he had an argument with Candace Branson, who had him thrown out. I cannot find another explanation than that he was the ghostwriter of the book and was either pitifully paid or wished to increase his fee when he saw the success of the latest book."

"Or she stiffed him."

He glanced at me and then back at the road. "Stiffed him?"

"You don't know everything, do you? Candace Branson is one of those people who can knock you over with overpowering friendliness. We know she lied about Bartholomew's manuscript. She seems like someone who might go back on a promise."

"You didn't warm to her, I fear."

"Laugh at me if you want to, but her behavior hasn't exactly been admirable."

"True. But she didn't know that Bartholomew was still in existence to be upset by her fake discovery. If he hadn't been turned, she'd have got away with it."

"And as his beneficiary, she'd make a nice chunk of change."

"But if we're to speak of behavior that's not admirable, don't forget your young friend likely murdered his employer."

I hadn't forgotten that. "I'm trying not to judge him before we've heard his side of the story."

"It all depends on whether he's in possession of the manuscript."

I nodded. I'd thought the same thing. And the fact that Karen had seen those mud-covered running shoes in her front hallway did suggest that Tristan Holt might have been with Candace. I told Lochlan about the shoes and that Giles Montague claimed to have overheard Candace speaking with a young American sometime in the night.

"Not compelling evidence but damning all the same."

"It seems so crazy to murder a woman to get a contract honored. Why didn't he hire a lawyer?"

"Perhaps he didn't have a contract. Perhaps it was Candace Branson's word against his. No doubt he'd signed a nondisclosure agreement."

"I hadn't thought about an NDA. Of course, that's the first thing she'd do. Let's say she tied him up legally. If he went public about their deal, he would break it. So she had him."

"It must have been a shock to see Tristan Holt at the book launch," he said, pulling smoothly around a pair of cyclists.

"And he went to see her that night. What do you bet she'd made it very difficult for him to gain access to her. She'd have thought she was safe all the way over here in Ireland. She'd never believe he'd follow her from Cleveland."

"And yet he did. And instead of fulfilling the contract, she had him thrown out of the party." He tapped his fingertips on the steering wheel. "Or did she really?"

I turned to him. "What do you mean? We both saw it."

"Maybe that was an act and they agreed to meet up later."

"In her room." I looked at him. "You're not thinking...?"

"Where mortals are concerned, I'll believe anything."

As the miles peeled away, my attention was increasingly taken by the beauty of the scenery. Lochlan's car was low and powerful, and it hugged the twisty road. I laughed with delight when I saw dolphins playing, watched over by soaring seagulls.

I could almost just sit back and act like a tourist except for the nagging feeling that a killer might be hiding out there somewhere.

We stopped first at Eagle Point, where there was a campground that housed both campers and tents. It seemed like a busy spot to me, but when Lochlan got out of the car, so did I. I came closer to him, and he turned. "Quinn, would you mind waiting inside the car with the windows rolled up? Just for a minute or two."

It was such a weird request, I asked why.

He looked slightly uncomfortable. "Your heartbeat and your, um, scent are muddling my senses."

"Right!" I said and pretty much ran around the side of the car and got in and slammed the door.

He walked away from the road and toward the camping park. He only went about ten feet. I could still see him. He was turning his head in a slow semicircle, scenting the breeze. He beckoned me, and I got out of the car. "There's a faint hint of him about a mile this way." He glanced down at my boots. "Will you come with me? Or would you prefer to stay here?"

I'd come all this way. I didn't want to stay stuck in the car while Lochlan got to have the whole adventure. Besides, I had seen Candace Branson's body. Whoever had done that to her ought to be punished. Lochlan's idea of punishment might be a little different from mine, and I was determined to be present when the culprit was uncovered so that I could call the Gardai.

We set off away from the busy campsites. There was no path, and the ground was uneven and rocky in parts. I was glad to have my sturdy boots as we strode along. I knew when we'd reached the site because Lochlan put his arm out and gently nudged me behind him. Stealthily, we trod forward. The vampire all but soundless. Me cracking a twig and banging my boot against a rock.

Soon we came to a clearing. Even I could see that the ground had been flattened and slept on recently. However, there was no sign of habitation now. "Was he here?"

"Yes. And not so long ago."

We began to search the area, looking for clues. I don't know what I expected to find. A confession? The missing manuscript?

Whatever he was, Tristan Holt wasn't one to litter. If I hadn't already known that someone had slept here, I would have walked by and not been any the wiser.

We'd turned around and headed back to the car when Lochlan stopped and bent down. He rose holding a slip of paper. I recognized it as one of the flyers advertising the book launch.

CHAPTER 13

"So he was here," I said as we looked at the brochure featuring *A Killer in His Sights* to be launched at The Blarney Tome in Ballydehag.

He nodded, and we headed back to the car.

I had that frustrated feeling you get when you run for a plane or a train or a bus and just miss it. You kept cursing fate. If only I hadn't wasted so much time trying to shove myself in trousers that no longer fit. If only we'd discovered Candace's body an hour earlier. We might have caught Tristan Holt red-handed.

Lochlan didn't share my frustration. "He's not left the area. We'll find him."

His cool assurance was irritating but also reassuring.

I clicked my seatbelt back on, and once more we headed down the ocean road. Twice more we stopped, and while I stayed in the car, Lochlan got out to do his bloodhound thing. Both times he got back in the car with a shake of the head.

But the third time, I could tell just from looking at him that he'd caught a scent of his quarry. He remained with his head raised in one spot, utterly still. Goosebumps rose on my arms. If I was Tristan Holt, I was certain I'd feel the hairs on the back of my neck start to rise.

I got out of the car without being fetched and came up beside Lochlan.

"Stay behind me. And don't speak. Stay as quiet as you can."

I nodded, and we set off. I stayed behind Lochlan, worried that my jangling heart and nervous sweat would get in the way of his tracking. I didn't see any evidence of tents or other people, but he remained on the course he'd set himself, striding off in virtually a straight line. I nearly screamed when a rabbit broke cover and ran right in front of me, but otherwise I managed to keep my mouth shut.

At length we came to a patch of flat ground beneath a tree.

In the clearing was a dark green pup tent that had seen better days. But more interesting than this was our quarry himself, sitting on a flat rock with his back resting against a tree trunk. He had a portable stove, and he was drinking coffee from a tin mug.

He was reading Bartholomew's latest book, appropriately named *A Killer in His Sights.*

"Good day to you, Mr. Holt," Lochlan said, sounding as pleasant as though they'd just bumped into each other on the high street of Ballydehag.

Tristan Holt nearly jumped out of his skin, splashing hot coffee on his bare hand, which made him curse and struggle to his feet. He looked surprised, angry, and guilty all at once.

"What are you doing here?"

"It's a fine day for a drive. Quinn and I decided, after the exertions of Bartholomew Branson's book launch, to take a day off. Have a bit of a holiday."

Tristan Holt didn't look thrilled to see either of us. His gaze darted between the two of us. He looked like he wanted to scamper away the same way that rabbit had done when I stumbled across it.

"I see you're staying in the area. Doing some touring of our fine coastline."

"It's not a crime."

"Bit of a gray area that, isn't it? You're meant to take advantage of the fine camping parks we have here in Ireland. Or, even better, you could have stayed in O'Donnell House. That's a beautiful bed and breakfast right in Ballydehag itself. No doubt you didn't know it was there. The proprietor's only recently opened it."

I almost felt sorry for poor Tristan. Lochlan was toying with him the way Cerridwen did if she was lucky enough to catch a moth.

"I couldn't afford it."

Lochlan looked puzzled. "Now that's a funny thing, isn't it, Quinn?"

Thanks for bringing me into this. Obediently I asked, "What is?"

"Wouldn't you think a young man who'd just come into some money would be able to treat himself to a nice bed and breakfast?" He looked significantly at the camp coffee. "Karen Tate does a lovely full Irish breakfast."

Tristan was wearing the same moth-eaten sweater he'd worn last night, and I suspected the full Irish breakfast was one in a long line of things that he hadn't indulged in since he'd arrived in the Emerald Isle.

He took a step forward. Foolhardy, I thought, given the size and cool menace of Lochlan Balfour. "Can I help you with something?"

I had to quell an urge to jump in front of him in case Lochlan went full-on vampire. But I should have known better. Lochlan was as smooth and icy as a glacier.

"I'm rather hoping you can help us. You see, Quinn and I know that Bartholomew Branson never left an unpublished manuscript."

His cheeks grew ruddy, and his jaw set. "So? What's that got to do with me?"

"Well, a great deal, I believe. Quinn feels, and I agree with her, that you might be the author of a mysterious manuscript that Candace Branson revealed to the world last night. After you left, that was, so you missed the excitement."

As I watched Tristan Holt, it was almost comical. I could see the pride of the author wanting to acknowledge his own work wrestle with the deal he'd no doubt made to keep his mouth shut. He settled on, "What makes you think I know anything about an unpublished manuscript by Bartholomew Branson? I never met the man."

Lochlan smiled. It wasn't a very friendly smile. "Let's just say it wasn't coincidental, us having the launch in Ireland. Quinn and I know quite a bit about Bartholomew Branson's literary estate."

I almost snorted. I knew way more about his literary estate than I ever wanted to. "There was no undiscovered manuscript. Was there?"

He shook his head. "I can't talk to you about this."

I stepped in now. I didn't know if we were playing good

human/bad vampire or what, but maybe it was time for a more sympathetic approach.

"I know you signed an NDA."

He looked at me sharply but didn't agree or disagree with me. However, I had his full attention. "I know you went to see Candace Branson last night at the bed and breakfast."

He didn't look scared now. He just looked mad. "Did she tell you that? What did she do, complain that I scared her? You saw her slap my face. Why would I go back for more?"

"Why did she slap you like that?"

He took a sip of coffee, and I thought he was buying himself time to think up a good reason. He came up with, "She misunderstood me. Thought I was coming on to her." He shook his head.

"Tristan. We know you went to see her last night. What did you do with the manuscript?"

"Nothing. She's crazy, and she's mean."

He finished his coffee and stomped over to the pot. "I'd offer you coffee, but I only have one cup."

I didn't say anything. If we stood here, he might keep talking. Sure enough, he said, "Anyway, if we did have a contract, and I'm not saying we did, and she never paid me the second half of what she owed me, and I'm not saying that she didn't, the way I figure it, the work reverts to me."

I was no literary attorney, and I wasn't remotely interested in who might or might not own his Branson knockoff. I wanted to know who'd killed Candace. "So you did see her last night. And before you try and argue that you didn't, I should tell you that your muddy running shoes were seen in the front hall by the door."

I glanced down significantly at the mud-encased running

shoes he was wearing right now. I had no idea if they were the ones that Karen Tate had seen, but he didn't know that.

"So what if I did have a meeting with Candace Branson? Is it a crime?"

Now bad vampire took over. He stepped close and loomed over Tristan Holt. "No. But murder is a crime."

The young author glanced at me with appeal and shock in his eyes. "What?" The word came out in a frightened whisper.

Since he'd asked me, I answered, "It's true. Candace Branson was murdered last night. Do you want to tell us what happened?" I pulled out my mobile phone. "Or do you want to wait for the cops?"

"Cops?" He looked around as though there might be a camera crew behind us and this was one of those shows where you make public fools of people.

Then he looked back at me and said, his voice trembling now, "You're serious."

"Who would joke about murder? Of course, I'm serious. Look, I don't think you're a killer, but you have to tell us what happened."

Okay, I did think he was a killer, but I'd seen that line on TV and it sounded really good.

He sipped his coffee, then tossed the rest on the ground and placed his cup carefully beside the coffee pot. He stood, put his grubby hands in his hair and squeezed as though he might be thinking about pulling tufts of hair out. "I didn't kill her. I wouldn't."

"Then you'd better tell us exactly what happened."

Tristan Holt looked seriously worried, as well he might. He'd confirmed that he'd been in Candace Branson's room the night she was killed. If he wasn't the murderer, he was probably the last person who had seen her before the murderer arrived.

All we needed now was to find the manuscript with him and they'd be slamming the cell door shut on Tristan Holt.

Lochlan glanced at me, and I knew we were having the very same thought. He said, "Quinn and I reckon that the person who has the manuscript is the one who killed Candace Branson."

I was looking at Tristan carefully as Lochlan said the words, and he looked ill. "Yeah, well, I don't have it. And you're not the police. Why don't you quit harassing me?"

Lochlan turned to me and said in a conversational tone, "He'd tell us to get off his property, but he's got no rights here."

I actually felt a bit sorry for the young man with dirt under his fingernails. I didn't think this was how he'd planned his Irish vacation.

The question was, how were we going to see inside his backpack? Or inside his tent? He wasn't exactly inviting us in.

Once again, Lochlan took over. "I have a mind to buy a little tent like this for myself. It must be very nice to wander around Ireland so unencumbered. Lightweight, is it?"

Tristan looked both shocked at the sudden change of subject and highly suspicious. As he should. "It's all right. It's old, though. You'll find much lighter ones now."

Lochlan strode towards the entrance. "Mind if I take a look?"

"As a matter of fact, I do."

But it was too late. The vampire was already unzipping the front fly and pushing his head and torso into the tiny space. It was almost comical. I could have told him that if he'd really been looking at buying a tent, he should look for something a lot larger.

"Hey! I don't want you in my stuff. Get out of there."

Lochlan emerged but, unfortunately for Tristan, or fortunately for us, he had Tristan's backpack in his hands.

The young author flew at the vampire and tried to tug it away from him, but Lochlan was bigger and stronger. He had the top of the bag open in mere moments and, looking at me with an expression of triumph, he pulled a familiar-looking sheaf of papers out of the pack.

"Care to explain?"

I was sorry to find we'd been right. I'd warmed to the young writer. I didn't want him to be a killer.

Tristan backed away now, suddenly bright red in the face. "That's my copy."

Lochlan shook his head. "I did say whoever had that manuscript was most likely Candace Branson's murderer."

"No. No, I tell you. I printed off a copy for myself. It's not the one she was showing off last night."

Lochlan looked at me with eyebrows raised. He might be a tech wizard, but a lot more of his existence had occurred before technology than after it. I nodded. If I was the author, I'd be carrying around a copy of the manuscript too.

"Give us one good reason to believe this isn't Candace's manuscript," I asked him.

He looked wild-eyed. "I can't. If I had my computer here, I could show you. But I didn't bring it with me. I'm traveling light. My laptop's back in Cleveland."

"How convenient."

Then I looked at him. "If your laptop was too heavy to

bring, what on earth are you doing lugging around a paper manuscript of a book? That has to be a lot heavier than most laptops."

"Okay. I'll tell you. And I'm breaking my nondisclosure agreement by talking to you about this at all," he said, as though that mattered now. I suspected that once the person you made a contract with was dead, the contract was pretty easy to break.

"Take us back to the beginning," I said. I suspected he needed a little bit of time to catch his breath and harness his wits so he could tell his story in a coherent fashion. It didn't look good for Tristan Holt, but I strongly believed in giving everyone the benefit of the doubt.

"I guess it started when I entered a writing contest. I've been writing all my life. I took creative writing in college and, even though I'm not a big fan of Bartholomew Branson, there was a contest with a couple of thousand dollars in prize money, and they promised that Branson's agent himself would read the novel. I was hard up for cash, I always am, but more important, I thought, what if I could get my work in front of Branson's agent? You have no idea how hard it is to get an agent to look at your work. So I entered the contest."

That sounded very much like something a university student in creative writing might do.

"Did you win?"

He shook his head. "I came in third."

"Bummer."

"I thought so. I got a hundred bucks, and somebody'd obviously read the manuscript because I got some nice comments back. I filed it away and forgot all about it until a couple of months ago. I got a call."

A couple of months ago, Bartholomew Branson had fallen off a cruise ship and supposedly drowned. "Who was on the other end of the phone?"

"You have to ask? Candace."

"Candace Branson phoned you?"

"Yes." He said it in a belligerent way. Like I might not believe him. Because I mostly didn't.

"What did she want?"

He began to bang his fist on the trunk of the tree he was leaning against. I doubted he even knew he was doing it. "She wanted to have coffee. She said she'd gone over the top entries in the Bartholomew Branson contest. At that point, he'd only been missing a couple of weeks, and I got the idea that she missed him so much, she wanted to talk to somebody who loved his work."

Was he really this naïve? And then I realized he couldn't be more than about twenty-three or -four. I'd probably been that naïve as well when I was that age.

"We had coffee, and she seemed a lot more interested in my work than in talking about her dead husband's. Finally, she asked if I'd be interested in a ghostwriting project."

"After one coffee date, she offered you a ghostwriting gig?"

"Well, she'd obviously already read the piece I'd submitted for the Branson contest. I had deliberately written something that I thought sounded like Branson. Not my usual voice at all. But for the two grand top prize money, I was willing to prostitute myself."

Now I began to understand. "That's what she'd loved about your work. That you could imitate Branson's work."

"It's not easy to write in another author's style. I was super proud of it. I really doubted that the casual reader would be able to tell which was his work and which was mine."

I wondered if she'd actually gotten the idea to continue Branson's work without him when she'd read Tristan Holt's submission. Even if Branson wasn't dead yet, she might have held on to the idea just in case.

"You agreed?"

He shrugged, suddenly looking a lot older than his age. "It was a twenty grand flat fee. Twenty grand meant I could take off some time and work on my own stuff. Plus, it wasn't that hard to copy Branson's style. If you can call it a style."

"So you took the twenty grand and you wrote the manuscript."

He shook his head, looking far from happy. "I took the five grand. It was five grand upfront, another five when I turned in the manuscript, and I'd get the final ten when the book got published."

I was no attorney, but it didn't seem like those were the greatest terms for Tristan Holt. What if the book had never been published? He'd have lost out on half his money. Echoing my thoughts, he shook his head and banged the tree trunk a bit harder. "I should have gotten a lawyer. But I didn't have any money, and she seemed like such a nice lady."

I knew only too well how enthusiastic and nice-seeming Candace Branson could be.

"Anyway, I finished the book. I turned it in. I waited for the second five grand. It didn't come. I phoned the number that Candace Branson had given me, and she never returned my calls. I emailed her. I emailed the lawyer who drew up the contract. Nothing."

He shook his head. "She stiffed me."

CHAPTER 14

"*T*hat must have hurt." I was trying to act sympathetic so he'd tell me more than he might have intended, but it wasn't difficult. I did feel bad for him.

"Then I saw the excitement build for Branson's last book. From the amount of press it was receiving, it was pretty clear that the book would hit every best-seller list just because it had Branson's name on it and the poor guy was dead."

"He's still a bestseller," I agreed.

"Then I saw that Candace Branson herself was coming over for this launch in Ireland. Probably I wasn't even thinking right, but I decided that if Candace Branson was going be here in Ireland, I would make sure to show up. I only wanted the money she owed me."

I could imagine being that angry. And it was a bold move.

"So you got on a plane and you came to Ballydehag."

"That's right. I found a dirt-cheap flight and I know how to live stealth camping. I was determined to get right up in her face. All I wanted was the five grand I was owed. But she was too cheap to pay it to me. First, she pretended she didn't even know who I was, so I told her I'd talk to Philip Hazeltine and Giles Montague if she didn't want to honor our agreement. She told me to come to the B&B where she was staying but no one could know. And, well, you saw the rest. She had me thrown out."

"So you admit that you did you go to the bed and breakfast late at night to see Candace Branson?"

"Because she told me to. When she threw me out, she said, 'We can't talk here. Come and see me later. I'm at the O'Donnell House, room three.'"

Maybe I'd half-believed a lot of his story. It was certainly plausible. But did he really think I was going to buy that Candace Branson had invited him to her room?

My skepticism must have shown on my face. For he said, "It's true. She even gave me her front-door key. How do you think I got in after hours?"

I looked at Lochlan. His story did sort of make sense. Lochlan shrugged.

I turned back to Tristan. "Well, pretend I believe you. Then what happened?"

"She'd told me to wait until everyone was in bed and the lights were out. She didn't want an audience, obviously. A little after midnight, I let myself in. I went upstairs and found room three, the one at the front of the house. When I went in, she was reading the manuscript. She had these glasses on and, I don't know, she just looked really pretentious. She said, 'Before this can be published, I'll have to do a lot of work. Frankly, it's pretty much going to be a complete rewrite. Be glad I'm not asking for the whole advance to be returned.'"

"She did?" That was harsh and, I suspected, untrue.

"I was furious. Nobody had asked me for revisions. And

our deal was twenty grand for writing the manuscript. Which I had done. She shoved a copy of *A Killer in His Sights* at me and told me to be thankful for the five thousand dollars and that maybe we could work together again in the future."

"Wait, you're saying she stiffed you out of your fee and still strung you along for more work?" That was the craziest thing I'd ever heard. But somehow, I suspected Candace had been capable of that kind of behavior.

"I don't get mad very often, but I was mad. I told her I wasn't leaving until I got my money. She threatened to call the police. I told her to go ahead."

"And then you strangled her?" Lochlan put in sweetly.

"No! She told me to look in her handbag and take whatever euros were in there and she'd send me a check when she got home."

Oh, this was not going to end well for poor Tristan. "You went through her handbag? And we're supposed to believe she was still alive when you did it?"

"She was. She told me to take the cash that was in her purse, since she'd be going home soon anyway. Then she said to contact her when I got back to the States."

"How much money was in her purse?" Lochlan asked.

"Six hundred euros and some change."

"Not five thousand dollars then, was it?"

"What was I going to do? It was the middle of the night. I don't know anybody in Ireland. I figured my best bet was to take the money and wait till I got home."

There was silence. I could just smell the scent of the sea and hear the sound of the odd car that traveled along the Wild Atlantic Way.

As though he couldn't stand the silence any longer, he almost shouted, "She was alive. I left and she was alive."

"What was she doing when you left?" Lochlan asked him. Oh, good question.

"She picked up the manuscript again and went back to reading it." He made a face as though he was suddenly in pain. "I couldn't stand watching her read it, especially with that look on her face, like she was about to puke from how bad it was."

His hands fisted as he spoke. No doubt he was unaware he was doing it, but considering the way Candace died and that he'd admitted to being in her room late at night and going through her handbag, the gesture only added evidence that he was guilty of murder.

"And then I left."

There was a beat of silence. "I can see that you're a fine novelist," Lochlan said. "You've spun a brilliant story there. I'll trouble you to tell it again to the Gardai."

He picked up his cell phone and, before I even knew what was happening, Tristan Holt ran at me, shoved me so that I tumbled back against Lochlan, who dropped his phone. In the time that it took us to pick ourselves up off the ground, the author was speeding away on foot, clutching his backpack to his chest.

"Are you all right, Quinn?" Lochlan asked.

"Yes. Fine. But we'll have to chase after him."

To my surprise, the vampire shook his head. "I don't think so."

"But he'll get away. He probably killed Candace Branson. And even if he didn't, he'd be a key witness."

Lochlan was watching the figure get smaller and smaller. "I'm curious to see where he goes."

"Then don't you think you should follow him?"

He shook his head. "I can find him well enough when I need to. He's a bag of nerves, and he's running on adrenaline. Very easy to track."

Right.

"But why are you letting him get away?"

He looked at me. "Before I make a grab at that young scribbler, I want to talk to Bartholomew Branson."

I turned so quickly, my head spun. "Do you still think Bartholomew killed his ex-wife? When you sent those two undead minders to stay with him?"

"He ditched them."

"What?"

"They were as surprised as you are. We'd all forgotten that the man spent his career writing about secret agents escaping from captors. He must have used the plot of one of his books, but he certainly hoodwinked Francis and Allan."

"Guess they're in the doghouse."

"You've no idea. You saw Bartholomew. He was very angry when he left us, and he spent most of the night alone. I'm curious to hear what his movements were."

"Will he tell you the truth?"

Lochlan sent me a cool glance. "Oh, yes."

Lochlan was still holding the manuscript. He read the title aloud. *All Fall Down.* I wouldn't have thought that was enough to kill for."

"It's not the book. It's the money that the novel will earn. A lot of people would be very happy to cash Bartholomew Branson's royalty checks." Including Bartholomew Branson.

"Him running away doesn't look good."

"No. Should we call the Gardai and report that we've seen him?"

He gazed at the pup tent, which looked even more forlorn now, as though it knew it had been abandoned. "We could, of course, but how helpful is it now he's run off again?"

Looking at the pup tent and his abandoned stove made me weirdly worried about Tristan Holt and where he was going to sleep that night. "Six hundred euros won't get him very far."

Lochlan looked at me curiously. "You believed him, didn't you?"

"You know, I think I did."

We both turned to stare in the direction that Tristan Holt had gone. I said, "If he was good enough to write a whole conspiracy thriller, when asked about his movements last night, wouldn't you have thought he'd have come up with a better story? That's what makes it sound like the truth."

Lochlan said, "There's something in what you say. But there's a lot of evidence stacking up against him."

"I know. And I have an idea."

"What's that?"

"Let's go back. You try to prove that Tristan Holt did murder Candace Branson, and I'll try to prove that he didn't."

He looked rather amused at my suggestion. "Is there a prize for the winner?"

I shook my head at him. "Only the satisfaction of helping the course of justice."

"I know you've Irish in you somewhere, Quinn, but it's deeply buried. You can't challenge a man like that without there being a proper wager."

This was ridiculous. "What did you have in mind?"

He seemed to think about it. "Since this is a crime apparently about greed, the wager should be a monetary one."

I felt sick deep in my belly. It was okay for Lochlan Balfour, who was I had no idea how many times a billionaire, to casually toss out the idea of a monetary bet. He could afford to lose. But what about me? I was a mortal, with a mortal's savings.

"What did you have in mind?"

"I think ten euros should do it."

I nearly fainted with relief. Ten euros was about fifteen bucks. I thought I could handle losing that sum. And, if I did happen to win, I wouldn't feel embarrassed to be taking that much money off someone else, even if they did have untold wealth. We shook hands on our bargain and decided we should head back.

Lochlan would have put the manuscript in the back of his car, but I took it from him instead. While he drove, I read Tristan Holt's manuscript in imitation of Bartholomew Branson. Lochlan was very easy company. He left me alone to read, not asking every five minutes what I thought of the book, which I knew I would be doing if I were driving and he were reading. And soon, I found myself falling into the story. I read for about half an hour probably, then looked up to find I was missing some of the most beautiful scenery in Ireland. I knew enough now anyway that I could stop reading, enjoy the scenery, and finish the book at my leisure.

"He's really a very good writer," I said at last.

"Does he sound like Bartholomew Branson?"

I screwed up my face as I considered. "Honestly? His biggest problem is that he's a much better writer than poor

Bartholomew. His prose is smoother, his sentences aren't so jerky, and already the protagonist is feeling more like a human being than a cartoon character."

"It'll be interesting to see what you think when you get to the end of the book."

Unlike reading one of the real Bartholomew Branson thrillers, I was actually looking forward to getting back to this one.

As we got closer to Ballydehag, he said, "Are you in a hurry to go straight back to your cottage?"

I wasn't nearly ready. I was having fun trying to solve this murder. I said, "Why? What did you have in mind?"

"For either of us to win our wager, we need to know more about Candace Branson's movements and more particularly, her visitors' after she returned to the bed and breakfast last night."

I glanced at him. "You're going to a lot of trouble for ten euros."

"I always find it isn't the amount wagered that's interesting, it's the bet itself."

Since I wasn't much of a betting woman, I couldn't comment.

He was right though. It really did seem like this murder revolved around money and greed. Which brought me to the obvious question. "Who benefited if Candace Branson died?"

CHAPTER 15

*H*e nodded. "An excellent question. And one I hope we'll soon have the answer to."

"Would Bartholomew know who Candace's beneficiary is?"

"The trouble with Bartholomew is that he's not a credible witness at the moment."

I nodded. "Because he's a suspect too. And, by the way, if we start trying to prove Bartholomew killed his wife, then that's one crisp ten euro note for me."

His lips quirked at that. "What will you do with your grand winnings, if you do win?"

I settled back and watched a seagull soar and dip. "Oof, that's a hard one. So many choices. I could have one glass of wine at the pub. I could afford both a coffee and one of the potato scones at the coffee shop."

"You'd blow it all at once then? You're not the type to save for a rainy day."

I nearly burst out laughing. I'd always been taught growing up that you should save ten percent of everything you earned. Which sounded great in a book or on a public television series, but the reality was money was a lot easier to spend than it was to save. Especially if you didn't have a whole lot of it. The idea of carefully saving some percentage of my ten euros made me laugh.

When we drew up in front of O'Donnell House Bed and Breakfast, he turned off the engine and looked at me. "We'll need a strategy."

"Right. You're trying to prove the young author is a killer who strangled Candace Branson, while I'm trying to prove he didn't."

"Exactly."

"What do we do? Ask the opposite questions?"

"Or ask different people questions and compare notes later."

I liked this idea. It seemed efficient and unbiased.

I knocked on the door, and when Karen answered it, she looked as frazzled as I've ever seen her.

"I don't know what I'm going to do, Quinn. I've had police up and down all day, carting that poor woman away, and then forensics going over the front room with a fine-tooth comb, and every time I turn around, there's a television blaring the *Antiques Roadshow*. I'm about ready to take a sledgehammer to every television in the place."

I had a sneaking feeling that might be the only way she was going to get that television program out of her house. I felt terrible that this was partly my fault. I'd thought I was so smart casting a spell that would prevent *Antiques Roadshow* from playing at all, but I'd made the worst rookie mistake. I'd cast the spell right in front of a vastly older and much darker witch. Most of us lived by the rule to do no harm. Biddy, however, had done so much harm she'd been given the death sentence. And while I was well aware that a lot of innocent women had been hanged and burned for witches over the centuries, it stood to reason that some of them must have deserved punishment, and I strongly suspected that Biddy O'Donnell was one of those.

She'd reversed my spell as easily as I'd made it but had been smarter than I was, as I couldn't reverse it back again.

There had to be a way to stop this. I'd give Biddy a stern talking-to and one more chance to mend her ways, and then I was going to have to go to Pendress Kennedy. I knew that Pendress would have a fit if she discovered that Biddy O'Donnell was not back in her underground prison but haunting O'Donnell House and once more making trouble for the citizens of Ballydehag. So far, she hadn't killed any husbands, but I couldn't rule out the possibility that she was the one who'd killed Candace Branson.

Karen looked surprised and somewhat flustered to see Lochlan standing at her door. But he was smooth as always and apologized for bothering her, saying he'd heard of her troubles and was there anything he could do to help?

"Perhaps you could help entertain the troops. They're all in the front room," she said. "At least they were. I've given up. I can't stand to go in there. The tension's dreadful. The detectives have asked them all to stay put. And what do you think that will do to my online reviews? First a murder in my house, and now it's being used as a veritable prison."

"I'm so sorry," I said, not knowing what else I could offer. "Can I help you with anything?"

"No. Go and talk to the prisoners. Maybe you can cheer them up. Oh, wait, Philip's not in the front room. He and

Irving had words, and then I heard him say he had work to do and he stomped up the stairs."

You didn't have to be a witch to feel the oppressive atmosphere pervading O'Donnell House. Lochlan told me he'd go into the front room, and I said I'd tackle Philip. Karen told me that Philip's room was across the hall from Candace's. I wondered if he'd heard anything during the night. Giles had claimed to hear voices from his room next door, but Philip hadn't corroborated or refuted his story.

I went upstairs, forcing my lead feet to climb, knowing that some of the essence of Candace Branson's spirit would still be hanging around. Besides, there was still some activity going on as the forensics team went over the room where she'd breathed her last.

I was glad to know that forensic technicians were across the hall in case I was about to closet myself with a murderer. Philip had every reason to do away with Candace. I'd seen his face when he discovered he wasn't going to be the agent for Bartholomew Branson anymore. Naturally, he'd argue that he'd only just found out this morning, after she was already dead, but I didn't believe it. If his room was right across the hall? The way Candace and Irving talked to each other, their voices booming, if they'd talked about Irving being Candace's agent, he'd have heard every word.

I could picture him sitting in an armchair reading a potential client's manuscript and then overhearing Candace and Irving making their noisy plans. Waiting until Irving had left and quietly slipping into her room. Maybe he'd tried to reason with her and then lost his cool and strangled her. Or perhaps he wasn't the killer. But if not, wouldn't he have heard Candace and her killer?

I hesitated before I knocked. It seemed very intrusive to go into the agent's room, not to mention dangerous. However, even if the techs didn't protect me, I had only to yell and Lochlan would be up here in a shot. Besides, I had plenty of power up my sleeve. And I was already on my guard. All in all, I didn't think I had too much to worry about, but still, I took a moment to center myself and recite a quick protection spell. Then I knocked.

"Come in." The voice sounded impatient. This was a man who had intended to be back in London by now and, regardless of the circumstances, didn't appreciate being held up. Besides, this whole trip now turned out to be not only a huge waste of his time but a humiliation as well. No wonder he wanted to get out of here ASAP.

He looked quite surprised to find it was me asking to be let in. "Miss Callahan. I assumed you were the detectives back to ask more questions."

"No. And please, call me Quinn. Could I come in?"

He was dressed the way he probably was Sunday afternoons in his home. He wore a buttoned-up cardigan sweater over woolen slacks, and on his feet were leather slippers.

"Of course. This is a surprise." From his tone, it didn't seem like it was the best surprise he'd ever had in his life.

"I'm sorry to bother you. Were you working?"

He gave me a thin smile. "My dear, a literary agent is always working. How can I help you? Have you a novel you're working on? Working with books all day, I can imagine you might secretly harbor hopes of publication yourself."

"No." I laughed awkwardly. "Nothing like that." Now that I was here, I didn't know how to begin. It was very difficult to ask a complete stranger if they had killed a woman. And it was only slightly less difficult to ask a complete stranger if they'd eavesdropped on a woman in the hotel room across the hall. I settled on, "I didn't want to sit with the others downstairs. It's kind of tense down there."

He might have wondered why I'd bothered coming back at all then, since I wasn't staying here, but as I had hoped, he was so caught up in the drama in the bed and breakfast that he probably hadn't paused to consider what I was doing back here.

"I couldn't stand it myself. I might have behaved in a very ungentlemanlike manner to our American friend."

Great, he was giving me the opening I'd hoped for. "I can't believe Candace Branson would choose someone like Irving to be her literary agent over you." I walked into his room when he held the door wider, and he returned to the chair he'd been sitting in, part of a nice little bistro set by the window. I sat opposite him.

As I'd guessed, he was working. A manuscript lay on the tabletop.

The sour smile hardened on his face. "I discovered Bartholomew Branson and encouraged him, shaped his career. And as for the things I did for Candace Branson..."

That made my ears perk up. "Candace? Did you have contact with her?"

"More than I'd ever have wanted in a lifetime. When they were married, she was perfectly ghastly. Constantly ringing up, demanding that he should get higher advances or more advertising, better placement in the bookstores, more media attention, spots on late-night talk shows—her demands were endless. She treated me like a genie who could magically grant all her wishes. Though she certainly didn't stop at three."

"I heard her say she was his business manager."

He laughed at that. One of those low, bitter laughs when you don't think something's at all funny. "There was nothing business-like about Candace Branson. She was driven by greed and always wanted more money. That was the only part of the business that interested her."

"I got the feeling that Bartholomew Branson made good money from his books. How much could she possibly need?"

He shook his head at me. "Some people have an endless craving. However much they have, they want more. Her appetite for money was insatiable."

I thought about poor Tristan Holt getting screwed out of half his advance. She hadn't spent much of her vast wealth on honoring her commitment to him. "What did she spend her money on?"

He shook his head again. "Mansions, jewelry, shopping. She wanted the best of everything. But at some point, I don't think it was about what she could have anymore because she could pretty much have had anything. She became like a drug addict, and money was her drug. After they were divorced, Branson used to call me absolutely beside himself because she kept threatening to take him back to court to increase her alimony. He didn't want the negative publicity, so then it was him always asking for higher advances." He shuffled the pages together and put them into a neat stack. "Not that she was the only one spending the money. Bartholomew Branson liked the good life as much as his ex-wife did."

Now that he was talking, I asked the question I'd really

come here to ask. "Giles said he heard someone in Candace's room last night. Did you hear anything?"

He leaned across the table as though we were in a busy restaurant and he didn't want to be overheard. "I don't want you thinking I was pressing my head to the wall, water glass to my ear, like in some corny, old film."

"No, no," I hastened to assure him. "I was wondering if, your room being so close to hers, you might have overheard something."

"She had a phone call."

That didn't seem very exciting. "She did?"

"Yes. About two in the morning, that would have been. I only know that because the ringing woke me."

"Who phones people at two in the morning? Did she answer it?"

"She did. Talked for about fifteen minutes. Sounded quite excited."

Huh. "Any idea who was on the other end of the phone?"

He shook his head. "Curiously, the police haven't found a mobile."

That was curious. As though the killer didn't want the record of Candace Branson's calls and texts easily available. They had to know that the police would be able to obtain the records.

"And then there was the American."

"Right. That young guy. Karen mentioned that she'd seen his shoes, and Giles said he heard him in Candace's room."

He shook his head. "I didn't hear that. But..."

He looked away from me, out the window into the garden, where late-summer roses bloomed against the rock wall.

"But?"

"It will sound crazy to you. It sounds crazy to me, and I can't believe I'm even telling you this, but I thought I glimpsed Bartholomew Branson in the garden late last night." He grimaced. "It sounds mad, I know. I got up for the toilet and, on my way back to bed, decided to open the window a trifle, as it was warm. That's when I saw him. Though I suspect I'd been dreaming and, given that we'd launched his novel, only thought it was him. Still, it rattled me."

And it was seriously rattling me. If Bartholomew Branson had been at O'Donnell House late last night, as furious as I'd seen him, I might win my bet with Lochlan, but it would give me no satisfaction to collect my winnings.

"Did he do anything?" Like climb into Candace's bedroom window?

"No. I only caught a glimpse of him crossing the lawn. As I said, it was probably a dream."

"Did you hear or see anything else?" I asked.

"I heard whispering a couple of times. Impossible to say who it was. For all I knew, she was talking to herself."

"Did you visit her room?" I tried to ask it in the most casual manner, as though they were neighbors in the B&B. Old friends who hadn't seen each other in a while. Why wouldn't he?

He was looking out the window, as though reliving his strange vision of the night before. "No. I didn't visit Candace Branson's room. Had no reason to," he said at last.

The words came out in a slightly higher pitch. I suspected he was lying.

I had all the answers to my questions and no more reason to stay here, and the agent was beginning to send pointed glances to the manuscript I'd interrupted him in the middle of reading. Just in case it was Candace's manuscript as ghost-written by Tristan Holt, I asked, "Is that the next J. K. Rowling?"

"Probably not." And, giving me a hard look, as though he knew perfectly well why I was asking, he held up the manuscript so I could see the front page. *The Magician's Garden* by Daphne Keene. *A Novel for Children.*

Not the next Bartholomew Branson, then.

CHAPTER 16

I went downstairs and found Lochlan chatting idly to Karen, clearly ready to go.

"How's it going down here?" I asked Lochlan and Karen. They both grimaced.

"I now understand why Karen's refusing to go into the lounge. Irving is loudly complaining that he needs to get back to New York."

Lochlan looked over at Karen, who nodded and added, "And Giles is coldly, fastidiously polite to Irving. He's made it very clear to the police that he'll cooperate but also wants very much to get back to his office in London. Chloe's put on earphones and is spending all her time on her laptop computer, no doubt pretending she's back in Dublin."

She glanced up towards where Philip was still working in his room. "Is he all right up there?"

"Seems to be. He's working."

She nodded. "I'll make him some coffee and take it up." Then she hesitated and said, "Quinn, come with me into the kitchen. I want your advice on something."

I looked at Lochlan with a silent question, and he nodded, telling me to go ahead.

I followed Karen into the kitchen. The world might be chaos, but her kitchen was spotless, and she was obviously managing the extended stay of her guests quite well. I'd half thought she might want to hire me as a waitress or something when I wasn't busy at the bookstore, but to my surprise, she walked me over to the back of the kitchen by the window that looked over into the backyard. She dropped her voice and said, "There was a set of Victorian kitchen scales sitting right there."

I obediently looked at where she was pointing, and all I saw was a shelf that had nothing on it.

I didn't say anything because I wasn't exactly certain what she was getting at. She picked up one of the crystal salt and pepper shakers that she put out with the breakfasts and put it down again. "I could take you all around O'Donnell House and show you where other things have gone missing." She looked truly distressed. "Quinn, I think one of our guests is stealing from me. This has all been so horrible, and now I'm not only dealing with murder but petty theft?" She turned to me, and her brown eyes looked wide and glassy, like a woman suffering from shock.

"Oh no," I said, but I knew it wasn't one of her guests stealing from her. Someone was stealing from her though, and I was pretty sure it was my not nearly long enough lost relative, Biddy O'Donnell.

She began rearranging her salt and pepper shakers. I didn't even think she knew what she was doing. "It's that damned television show. Playing constantly with all those antiques and telling the world how much they're worth now."

I knew she was right. And I felt terrible because it was my fault that no other program would play. I'd been tricked by Biddy so that my spell was reversed.

"That's why I wanted your advice. I don't know what to do. Should I tell the police?"

"Oh, no, don't do that," I said in a panic.

She nodded. "That was my instinct, too. But what if the same person who is stealing my antiques is also a killer? And I never said anything to the police? Wouldn't that make me guilty too? An accessory after the fact or something?"

I shook my head vigorously. "No. It wouldn't even be the same police investigating. A little petty pilfering is a long way from murder."

"But I keep thinking, what if Candace Branson caught the thief red-handed? They could have been taking things from her room when she walked in. And they panicked and killed her."

It wasn't the worst theory I'd ever heard, except for the fact that I was a hundred percent certain I knew who the thief was. I said, "Do you really think a top literary editor and two successful agents would stoop to petty thievery? And Chloe is always on her laptop computer. I don't think she even looks up at the TV."

She tapped the side of her nose. "Kleptomania is a serious disease, Quinn. It's not about need. It's a kind of addiction. I saw a program about it once."

She was probably right. And I knew who had it.

And yet... What if she was right? I was so certain that Biddy O'Donnell was behind the thefts, but what if it was one of her guests? And I was perverting the course of justice? I tried to think. "What about your shop? Has anything gone missing from there?"

"I don't think so. Not that I've noticed. I haven't been today, though, obviously. I had a friend watch the shop for me today. She wouldn't know the stock well enough to be able to tell if anything was missing, though."

"Well, all your guests are stuck here for the moment. Is anything gone that was extremely valuable?"

She shook her head. "A few things were sentimental though."

"My advice is to do nothing for the moment. Anything that you feel is valuable or sentimental, I would put in your shop, maybe tucked away in the storage room. Replace the items with things that have no value, or little value, and certainly not sentimental value to you."

"Yes, that's a good idea. I'm so glad I had someone to talk to. It's awful serving tea and biscuits and breakfast with a smiling face while all the time worrying that I'm housing a thief."

I didn't say it, but more frightening was that she was probably housing a murderer.

Then I said, "How are you managing?"

She grimaced. "This wasn't how I thought running a B&B would turn out. But on the bright side, I'll make a good bit of money in my first month now that they've all had to stay on."

"What about upcoming bookings?"

"Too early to say. I've got a few weeks booked and no one's canceled yet, but then of course the news hasn't traveled far yet."

She'd stretched out the yet, and I understood what she meant. Hopefully the news that Bartholomew Branson's widow had been killed would be the story that traveled to the United States and wherever else his readers had been. And the specific location of the murder would hopefully not be widely reported.

Having calmed her down, I headed out to where Lochlan was patiently waiting for me by the front door. We said goodbye to Karen and left.

I waited until we were back in the car before I told him everything. He knew better than anyone what Biddy was capable of. She'd wrapped my entire cottage around with impenetrable thorns like I was some middle-aged Sleeping Beauty when she was in a temper tantrum. I was sure she'd steal from Karen without a second thought. "What am I going to do? I've got to shut this down."

"You're certain Biddy O'Donnell is stealing Karen's antiques?"

"The old witch is obsessed with the *Antiques Roadshow*. In her day, a penny would probably buy you a castle. Now she sees that old everyday items are worth so much money, she's delighted."

"But how is she selling them? She can hardly go into Karen Tate's store and try and sell her back her own goods."

"I don't know. But I'm going to find out. Did you find out anything in the front room?"

"I can tell you that those two men, Giles and Irving, have no love for each other. If there's another homicide, it will likely be agents or editors killing each other out of professional jealousy. The young woman's ignoring both of them, but I suspect she stays in the front room to keep an eye on them."

"Good for her. We really need to get this thing wrapped up."

I hesitated to do it, but he had to know, so I told him about Philip spotting Bartholomew out in the garden the night before.

He didn't look surprised or shocked, more resigned. "I'm going to have a quiet word with Bartholomew Branson. If he's taken to killing people, he'll have to find a new home. Devil's Keep is a safe refuge for our kind, but it won't remain so if it harbors murderers."

As his closest neighbor, I was very happy to hear that. "Philip also said that Candace got a phone call around two in the morning."

Lochlan glanced at me. "Did she take the call?"

"She did. And he thinks she spoke for ten or fifteen minutes."

"That's interesting."

"I thought so too," I said. "Who calls someone in Bally-dehag at two o'clock in the morning?"

"When it happens to me, it's usually an international call. They forget to calculate the time zones correctly."

Since I'd been woken more than once by one of my friends in Seattle who had that very issue, I agreed with him. "Now we need to find out who she was talking to in the middle of the night. According to Philip, her mobile's missing."

"I'm sure the police can get hold of her phone records. It just takes time."

"And we need to find out what Bartholomew was doing there."

"I'm going to find out." His voice sounded steely and very

annoyed. I reminded him that Bartholomew hadn't killed his ex-wife. Probably.

"It doesn't matter, Quinn. He can't show himself to mortals. He'll put all of us in a very difficult position."

I hadn't thought about that. "What happens when a mortal finds out about you?"

He sent me a sharp look, and I said, "Normal mortals. Not people like me."

"We have ways of erasing people's memories. But we'd prefer not to do it. There's always a risk the memory loss will be permanent."

Good to know.

"So if Bartholomew had accidently been seen by his ex-wife, he could have made the problem go away?"

He tapped his fingers on the steering wheel. "We could. But he probably didn't know that."

Darn it, that put Bartholomew Branson back at the top of the suspects' list. "But Philip only thought he saw Bartholomew on the grounds. And we have to remember it was dark. That really doesn't prove he was there."

"No, it doesn't. But if Bartholomew Branson was there, I will find out."

"I don't know. What did he really have to gain? I mean, to give the dead woman credit, she was definitely pushing to keep his name and his legacy alive. For a guy that craves fame the way he does, maybe that would have been a good thing."

He didn't look convinced. "He was furious when he found out. He wants to write his own posthumous manuscripts, don't forget."

As we grew closer to the castle, I said, "You could just drop me at the cottage."

He turned to me. "You're deep in this, Quinn. I want you to be there when I talk to Bartholomew. With you there, he may be more inclined to tell us the truth."

I'd never thought I was the kind of person that encouraged truth-telling, but okay. We entered the castle, and it was like the party had never existed. Everything had been cleared away so efficiently. I'd have asked for the name and number of his cleaners, except I doubted very much I could afford them.

He strode up the stone stairs, and I followed. Bartholomew was sitting in the castle library reading, appropriately, *A Body in the Library* by Agatha Christie. It was the next selection in our vampire book club.

Oscar Wilde was sitting in the other chair reading Alexander Pope. He glanced up at Lochlan bearing down on Bartholomew and then at me and said, "Oh dear. Has somebody been a naughty vampire?"

Before Bartholomew could answer, Lochlan was in his face. "I hope you've got a good explanation for why you were seen at O'Donnell House last night?"

Bartholomew looked suddenly nervous, his gaze darting between me and Lochlan. "I didn't do anything."

"And yet you went there against my express orders. You were seen."

He put his book down and leaned back, closing his eyes. "Oh, man. I'm not used to this undead thing. I was hot under the collar, I admit it. I went over there intending to talk some sense into Candace, not that I could ever do it. Maybe I just wanted to give her a good scare." He held up his hands. "Before you lay in on me, I know I'm not allowed to do that. And I caught myself in time."

I didn't believe him. Maybe it was my witchy senses or he was a really bad liar, but I did not believe him. I stepped forward. "That's not true. You were seen inside O'Donnell House."

Lochlan flicked a gaze my way but didn't say a word. In the same way I had known Bartholomew was lying, he knew I was.

However, my bluff worked. The author turned vampire got all huffy and said, "I swear I didn't kill her."

"But you did go in O'Donnell House. If you didn't kill her, what were you doing in there?" I asked.

"I waited until she was asleep. I only wanted to see the manuscript. See if this guy she hired was any good. If I didn't like it, I was going to swap out his manuscript for mine."

"You were going to what?" I yelled. "Do you have any idea how dangerous that would be? You're dead, Bartholomew. You have to stay dead."

"I know, I know. But don't forget I was married to that woman for more years than I care to recall. Believe me, she's a snorer. I waited until she was full-on snoring and then I let myself into the room."

Even though I was furious with him, I was relieved. If Bartholomew had the missing manuscript, then Tristan had been telling the truth. I held out my hand. "Give me the manuscript."

He opened his eyes and his hands wide. "I don't have it. It wasn't there."

Oddly, now I did believe him. "The manuscript wasn't there? Are you certain?"

"Yes. I searched everywhere."

Which put Tristan, who definitely did have a copy of the manuscript, back on the hot seat.

"What time was this?" Lochlan asked. Oh, good question. I should have thought of that.

"About three a.m."

There didn't seem to be any more to be gained, so we left them reading. We went into Lochlan's office, and he shut the door behind us. Actually, it was more like a slam.

"This room's completely soundproof, it can't be bugged, and we can't be overheard. You can speak freely."

That was great, but I didn't know what I wanted to say. Except, "Did you believe Bartholomew?"

"Oddly, yes."

"So what on earth is going on? All along we've thought that Candace was killed because of that manuscript. But what if she wasn't? What if it was something else?"

"Such as?"

I shook my head. "I have no idea. But something's not making sense here. We have a B&B full of people who wanted that manuscript, and they all claim not to have it. Tristan Holt admits to visiting Candace Branson after midnight, and he had a copy of the manuscript, but he claims it was his own copy. As he's the author, it makes sense that he'd have one."

"Except, as you pointed out, if he didn't bring his laptop with him to Ireland because of weight, would he really cart about a sheaf of paper?"

"Then there's that. When Bartholomew searched Candace's room at three in the morning, the manuscript was gone."

"And if he heard her snoring, we know she was still alive."

"Right. Which means that Tristan Holt isn't our killer." I all but held out my hand for the ten euros.

"Not so fast. Who's to say he didn't come back again? Perhaps that was him calling her at two in the morning."

"You know what I think?"

He shook his head, looking amused. "What is it you think?"

"I think there are too many possible killers and too few people who don't have reason to lie to us, which makes it really difficult to find Candace's killer." I glanced at my watch. "And I should try to get a couple of hours of work in at the bookshop."

"You know Dierdre loves working there."

"That's nice, and I really appreciate the help, but I'm paid to work there. I don't want Lucinda to think I'm shirking."

"I'm sure Lucinda will be delighted with your profits this month. You've worked hard on the launch of Branson's novel. You deserve a little time off."

I stared up into his gorgeous face. "Seriously? You consider tracking a killer a holiday? If I take time off, I might like to go to Paris or spend a day at the spa. Not sleuthing."

"Duly noted." He picked up his car keys. "Come on. I'll drive you to the shop."

"Actually, drop me at home. I'll change into something a little more businesslike than yoga pants."

CHAPTER 17

The following day, I tidied the children's section, which left my mind free to puzzle over Candace's murder. We seemed to have arrived at an impasse. If she'd been murdered for that manuscript, then where was it? All I could think of was that the killer had disposed of it, realizing, after the murderous rage had passed, that holding on to that manuscript was the equivalent of waving around a smoking gun.

Even if they'd hidden it somewhere and retrieved it later, the minute that manuscript surfaced, whoever produced it was buying themselves a one-way ticket to jail.

There was something missing. I suspected the police were as confused as we were. Irving had been asked to remain a few more days while the police pursued their inquiries, but without hard evidence, they couldn't hold him. Irving being Irving, I was sort of surprised he hadn't gotten belligerent and demanded to leave, calling on his rights as an American. But he'd been remarkably easygoing about the delay. Why?

So many whys and not nearly enough becauses.

I reordered *The Lion, the Witch and the Wardrobe* series into the proper sequence, and then I heard the door open with a new customer. Before I turned to see who it was, I felt a chill. The hairs on the back of my neck didn't just rise; I felt as though a woodpecker was banging away on the top of my spine.

I rose to my feet, wincing a bit because I'd been too long crouched in the same position. I really needed to work out more. And as I turned, I found myself confronting Tristan Holt. No wonder my awareness had kicked into overdrive. And right now, my flight or fight response was following it. The scruffy, young guy with dirt under his nails might well be a vicious murderer of bookish women.

Since I couldn't think of a thing to say, I just stared at him. He stared back at me for a moment that seemed to last several thousand years. Finally, when I couldn't stand it anymore, I asked, "What are you doing here? The last time I saw you, you were running away."

That seemed to break the ice. He took a step forward. And I took a step back. He said, "I came back to help the police by telling them everything I knew about Candace. I told them I was in her room that night and—everything."

"That's the right thing to do. Good for you. But then why did you act so guilty yesterday?"

"I was just so shocked when you and the tall, scary dude came to my campsite, told me Candace Branson was dead and practically attacked me."

"To be fair, it wasn't really an attack. We just wanted to find out what you knew."

"Believe me, it felt like an attack."

I could see how that could happen, if he was innocent. "I'm really sorry if we startled you."

"Startled me? I didn't even know Candace Branson was dead. Then you're throwing accusations and suggesting that if I had the manuscript, I must be the murderer. I panicked. That's why I took off."

I felt guilty now. We'd scared him away from his temporary home. From the look of him, Tristan Holt hadn't spent the night at a Hilton hotel. He looked pale, exhausted and grubbier than the day before. "Did you go back and get your tent?"

He made a sound of derision. "No. I was scared you'd have more heavies waiting for me."

I was old enough to be his mother, and I couldn't stand the idea that I'd deprived him of his shelter. He must have slept under the stars last night. "Do you have a place to stay?" I wasn't going to put him up in my cottage. I might feel bad, but I wasn't suicidal. But I wondered if I could find him a place to say somewhere in Ballydehag.

He surprised me by saying, "Yes." Then his gaze dropped, and he looked a little embarrassed. "I'm on my way to O'Donnell House."

My eyebrows flew up at that. "You are? Do you know how much that place costs?"

"Philip Hazeltine is lending me the money until we get the manuscript sorted out."

"Philip Hazeltine?" I couldn't get my head around this.

"Yeah. After I ran away from you, I ended up at the beach. I sat there for hours trying to figure out what to do. I knew I had to talk to the cops, but then I figured, if Candace was gone, maybe Bartholomew Branson's agent would be interested in *All Fall Down*."

All I could think of was how cunning he was. If he had killed Candace Branson, his plan was breathtakingly simple and brilliant. With her death, and since the contract hadn't even been completed, as he hadn't received the second part of his payment, I was willing to bet the rights reverted to him. He was in a pretty good position. His story only had to be halfway good that somebody was going to pay a lot of money to publish it. So he'd approached Bartholomew Branson's agent. Nice.

Of course, he might not be the murderer, and then he got a little more credit for coming back to give what help he could to the Gardai, but the upside to himself was still very huge. His career was about to take off, and he had to know it.

And in visiting me? There could only be one reason. "You're looking for your manuscript back."

He shook his head. "No. I don't need it. I backed up to the cloud. All I need is internet and a printer."

"So why are you here?"

"I just wanted to tell you. In case we ran into each other or something. And besides, you were cool when I first arrived here and didn't know anybody. You invited me to the party."

I felt like he'd smacked me. "And by inviting you, I wonder if I started a chain of events in motion that ended up with Candace Branson's death." I could almost picture a line of dominoes, the last one being a little doll figure of her standing with the microphone announcing at the launch party that she had in her possession a brand-new Bartholomew Branson manuscript.

I wasn't sure why the ghostwriter being in attendance

would put her in more danger. I just had a sneaking suspicion that it had.

"Is it weird?" I asked him.

"Is what weird?"

"That you're staying in the bed and breakfast with agents who were fighting over that very manuscript and Branson's old editor."

He shook his head. "No. It's an incredible opportunity."

I looked at him. "You're a smart guy who just wrote a thriller full of twists and turns. Who do you think murdered Candace Branson?"

He looked serious and nervous all at the same time. "I honestly don't know. I didn't like her, and she totally stiffed me over my fee, but I hate thinking that somebody strangled her and stole my manuscript." He sent me a steely glare. "And let me be perfectly clear that it wasn't me who strangled her."

"It makes no sense," I said, repeating what I'd been saying in my own head all afternoon. "Why kill the woman for the manuscript? Anybody who knew what she was up to would figure out that the real author would have a computer file of the manuscript."

"My theory is that the killer didn't know there was a ghostwriter," he said. "I sat by the ocean most of yesterday afternoon thinking it all through."

I was so caught up in this whole conspiracy, I'd completely forgotten the obvious. "You're right. Most of the people at that launch believed it was a legitimate manuscript."

"It's not like Candace was bragging about the fact that she'd hired somebody to impersonate her dead ex-husband."

"So who did know? Who knew your secret?"

"She did, obviously. I did, even more obviously. And the lawyer who drew up the contract. I'm not sure anyone else was in on the plan."

"What about Irving? He and she seemed like they were pretty close. More than agent and client."

"Yeah. I picked up on that too. If she did tell him, I never knew anything about it. I only ever met with her and the lawyer who drew up the contract. He's still in New York. I checked."

"What about your lawyer?"

He pushed his hands into the pockets of his jeans. "I couldn't afford one. And I was stupid enough to trust her."

"I have to ask, who did you tell?"

He looked a little shifty. "I signed a nondisclosure agreement. I already told you that."

"I know, but this was a pretty big break. You must have told someone you knew you could trust. Your girlfriend? Your mother?"

"Becca Morley," he said in a low voice.

"Becca Morley? Who's she? And was she here on the night of the gala?" I felt like that was all we needed, yet another suspect in a complicated murder investigation.

He shook his head. "She's my critique partner back at home. I told her."

"You used a critique partner when you were ghostwriting for somebody else?" And I'd thought he was so smart.

He shook his head as though I was not so smart. "Obviously not. I just wanted to tell her."

The way he shifted from foot to foot and wouldn't meet my gaze gave me the answer right away. "You like her. You were trying to impress her."

"Maybe. Probably."

"Tell me about Becca Morley. Could she have told someone?"

"She promised she wouldn't, but how would I know if she had?"

"You need to find out. You're going to have to phone her and tell her what's going on. If there's any connection..." My words trailed away.

"It still doesn't make sense," he said. "If she told someone that I had written a fake manuscript, wouldn't I be the one who was in danger?"

"Oh, that's a good point. Except now you're the golden goose."

He didn't look thrilled. "The golden Bartholomew Branson goose. Yeah."

"The person who might want you dead is the real Bartholomew Branson," I said.

He laughed, understandably thinking I'd made a joke. "I don't think he's going to mind too much."

Oh, wouldn't he be surprised.

CHAPTER 18

I went straight home after work, needing time in my quiet cottage. My thoughts were racing around without form or structure. Everyone seemed guilty and no one. Was the manuscript the vital clue, or was it a wad of recycling?

Cerridwen happily polished off a dinner of gourmet cat food, and I, still smarting from the discovery that my hiking trousers no longer fit, grilled a piece of salmon I had in the freezer and served it with brown rice and spinach.

I brewed myself up one of my special teas for relaxation and clarity. I took it into the living room, which overlooked the ocean. I tried to settle, but I felt all the stress and horror of the last few days circling around me like noisy crows. I closed my eyes, breathed in and out slowly a few times. I was beginning to feel the wheeling crows settle when I was jerked out of my quiet by the television turning on.

I cried out, "Really? Really?"

"*...That's really a very fine example of British slipware. Of* course, you want to know the value. I would think at auction the cottage would fetch four hundred pounds."

"As much as that," a pleased-looking man said, grinning down at the brown and yellow pottery house.

I was about to flip off the TV when the camera zoomed in on a paper manuscript in a buff cardboard cover marked with ink scribbles and streaks of dirt. The book expert asked a tall woman in glasses to tell him how she happened to have a shooting script of *The Quiet Man*.

"Well, my great aunt was a typist for John Ford, the director, and she used to love to tell the stories of being on set for *The Quiet Man*. I think she had a terrible crush on John Wayne."

The book expert chuckled. "I'm sure she did. The Quiet Man *was, of course, filmed in Ireland in 1951. The film was released in '52, so this has been in your family quite some time. How exciting she got to meet the great actor himself.*"

"It was. She met all the cast. There's a picture of her with them in the box."

Then the camera panned in on a black and white photograph of an attractive woman beaming and surrounded by a group of people I didn't recognize and one I certainly did. There was John Wayne with his arm around the typist, grinning at the camera.

I put the remote control back down and settled back to watch.

"Anyway, when the filming ended, they didn't need the scripts anymore, and my auntie took one home. I didn't even know she had it. I found it in her papers when she passed away."

"My goodness, this is really something," he said. "It's a difficult thing to value. If John Wayne had signed it or her boss, John Ford, had signed it, it would be worth vastly more. John Ford won best *director for that picture. However, even as it is, just a curiosity, I think a film buff would pay fifteen hundred pounds for this. And if you had a few people competing, oh, it could go for two thousand pounds, maybe even twenty-five hundred."*

She looked tickled pink. *"It's more than my poor great-auntie ever earned typing, I can tell you that."*

They both had a good chuckle, and then suddenly I was looking at a Georgian silver tea service.

I flipped off the TV. "Biddy!" I yelled. There was no answer. "I want a word with you." I sensed she was gone, though I could still smell the faint scent of earth and mangy cat.

"Fine," I snapped. "You want to play hide and seek?"

I jumped up, got my candles and laid them out in a circle. Cerridwen saw what I was doing and immediately came over, sitting with me in the center.

"Biddy O'Donnell, wherever you be, Biddy O'Donnell, I summon thee," and then I pictured the nasty, old witch. I stared at the candle repeating the spell until I smelled her. She always smelled like she'd just been dug up. When she appeared in the middle of my circle, she did not look pleased. With her, naturally, was her familiar, Pyewacket, who took one look at Cerridwen and hissed. That knocked her head to one side but didn't make her any less aggressive.

"What did you do that for?" Biddy asked me.

I narrowed my gaze at her. I felt like arching my back and hissing, too. "Where is it?"

She looked completely baffled. "Where is what? I was nicely settled in my old home, about to find out what a set of silver would go for. When I think of the knives and spoons I owned hundreds of years ago, it's enough to make me spit. All

I had to do was bury them in the ground so I could dig them up again. They'd be worth a fortune today."

"I'm not interested in cutlery, and I think you know it. What did you do with the manuscript?"

"Manuscript? You mean like the monks have?"

"Stop toying with me, Biddy. You've been watching nothing but TV for months now. You know perfectly well what a manuscript is. And I think you took a manuscript from Candace Branson's bedroom in O'Donnell House."

She went sly and shifty on me, as she always did when she was caught out in wrongdoing. "She didn't want it, did she?"

"Why not?"

"Because she were dead."

I'd have smacked her if she wasn't so repulsive. "You saw what happened? You've seen us all running around trying to solve the murder of Candace Branson, and all the time, you knew who did it?"

"Don't get your shift in a twist, girl. I did not see who killed that woman. I didn't even know she was dead at first. I came in to watch a nice bit of telly, and she were lying there in the bed. I thought she was asleep. I put the telly on. It was that nice young man who does the china. Had a bit of Spode, he did. Then Pyewacket acted peculiar and began sniffing around at the woman, and that's when I realized she wasn't sleeping."

"But I could tell she was dead just walking up the stairs. Didn't you feel it?"

The old witch glared at me. "I was buried in the ground next to a graveyard for three hundred years. Me senses are dulled."

"Good point." I kept forgetting that she was a little bit undead herself. "You'd seen that episode already, hadn't you? The one where that woman had a script from *The Quiet Man.*" That's why she'd turned on my TV and then left. She didn't want to watch a rerun.

"What if I did? A thousand pounds for a bit of paper. Mad it was. I'd heard all the shouting and argumentation over the manuscript at my old house and thought it would be worth a nice bit of gold."

"You have interfered in a murder investigation." I tried to sound very severe, but she didn't look bothered.

"Oh my. What will they do? Hang me?"

Then, as though I had forgotten she had been hanged, she shifted her head around, putting it more firmly on top of her neck.

I was going to remind her that if she didn't behave, I was going to put her back under the yew tree where she'd been cursed to stay for so long, but it was a threat that was going to get pretty flimsy if I kept pulling it out every five minutes.

We both knew I couldn't do it on my own anyway.

Instead I tried to appeal, not to her good nature because she obviously didn't have one, but to her self-interest. "Karen is going to do very well with that bed and breakfast if you behave. But if this murder remains unsolved, she'll have to close it down, and she'll sell those comfortable beds that you enjoy so much and get rid of those TVs that are all tuned to your favorite show. Is that what you want?"

Her wrinkled and age-spotted lower lip protruded in a pout. "No."

"Fine. Where did you put that manuscript?"

She flounced over to my wardrobe, and before my astonished gaze, pulled open the doors and dug to the back of the cupboard where I stored the guest room sheets and blankets. From underneath, she pulled out the manuscript and handed it to me.

It was as though she'd handed me burning coals. I wanted to drop the pages rather than touch them. "You put that here? In my house? Don't you know the police are assuming that whoever is holding on to this manuscript is the person who killed Candace Branson?"

She looked somewhat interested at that. "Did you? Kill her?"

"No, I did not."

She gave me a knowing leer. "Come on, you can tell me. You won't be hanged for it. They don't do that anymore."

"The only reason the evidence is in my cottage is because you planted it there. I did not kill Candace Branson. Why would I?"

Once again, she gave me that knowing leer. "Sometimes the urge just comes over a body."

I took a step back. "It doesn't come over me."

She leaned over and patted my hand. "You're young yet."

I was gripping the manuscript in both hands, and her touching me just made me even more eager to drop the thing.

"That night, when the woman died and you took the manuscript, did you see anything significant?"

"Now, let me see." She leaned back and closed her eyes. "The painting of fruit and dead fish wasn't bad. And there were some lovely dolls, like the ones I used to have when I was a child. Of course, the clothes were terrible moth-eaten, but the little painted faces took me back."

"Not what did you see on the television. Did you see anybody come into her room?"

"No."

"Where was the manuscript?"

"Lying on the bed beside her. Though some of the pages had slipped to the floor, probably when she was being strangled."

"They were out in plain sight?"

"Aye. I just said."

"So she wasn't killed for the manuscript?"

I had no idea why I was discussing Candace Branson's death with Biddy. She wasn't interested in solving a crime. Not unless there was something in it for her.

The sly eyes focused on the pages in my hands. "What are ye going to do with it then?"

"Give it to the Gardai, I suppose." And how was I going to do that without giving them some explanation of how I'd come across it?

"Don't be hasty. There could be a fine profit to be made."

"But not by me." I glared at her. "Or you."

IT WAS STILL PRETTY EARLY in the evening, but I felt this news couldn't wait. After discovering I wasn't going to let her sell Tristan's manuscript, Biddy flounced off in a huff. And good riddance.

I called Lochlan and explained that it was Biddy who'd taken the manuscript. "So this whole time we've been chasing that missing manuscript, thinking whoever had it was the killer, and we were wrong. It was a red herring."

"Curious," he said, not all agitated like I was. But then Lochlan never seemed to get agitated. Maybe that's what living for eight hundred years did for you. Gave you perspective on the human condition. "Come to the castle. No one's gone out yet, so we can get the book club together for a quick meeting."

"Excellent." I really wanted other minds to talk over this new development with, since I wasn't eight hundred years old and I was seriously agitated.

When I got to the castle, Lochlan let me in and escorted me to the library. Bartholomew, Dierdre, Oscar, Thomas Blood, and Lady Cork were present. It wasn't the full book club, but that was fine.

I explained that the missing manuscript had been found at the back of my cupboard and briefly filled them in on the antics of Biddy O'Donnell.

"Biddy O'Donnell?" Thomas Blood said in his loud, blustery way. "I thought she was back in her underground prison."

"No." I left it at that.

"Fine woman in her day," he said.

"But anyway, now it seems we've been wrong thinking whoever killed Candace Branson stole the manuscript."

"Unless there's another copy," Bartholomew said.

I felt a headache forming. "We know Tristan Holt, the ghostwriter, had a copy with him. And Candace had one, which I also now have."

"Perhaps Candace shared the manuscript on a confidential basis before announcing its existence."

"Really? Why would she do that?"

"Quinn, I can see I need to explain to you how publishing

works," Bartholomew Branson said in a condescending tone. I tried to overlook the patronizing note because I really did need to understand more about his world if I was going to solve Candace Branson's murder, which was the quickest way of getting the police and a lot of nosy reporters out of Ballydehag.

I wasn't the only one who had secrets they preferred to keep to themselves. There were other witches in town, and the last thing Lochlan Balfour and the undead residents of the castle wanted was close scrutiny of their lives and, even more important, their identities. I was certain that Lochlan, high-tech wizard that he was, had given them all passably good documents and so forth. It seemed like the kind of skills he'd have, but I doubted he wanted them scrutinized by law and government agencies.

"Okay, explain it to me," I said to Bartholomew.

"It begins with the literary agent. If one has an agent, that is. The agent is the author's salesperson and to some extent a co-manager of their career."

"And how do you choose an agent?" I asked.

He chuckled. "Normally, it's the agent who chooses the author, unless the author is high-profile enough that agents come to him. Or her. But I was a young author sending out query letters and sample chapters to every agent I met, read about, or heard of. For the most part, those that deigned to reply rejected me. I tried every decent agent in New York, and then I turned to London agents. I got more rejections—"

"And still you didn't take the hint," Oscar said softly.

Bartholomew's hands fisted, but otherwise he pretended he hadn't heard the interruption. "Then Philip Hazeltine replied. He said he thought I had something and worked with me until he felt the novel was good enough to send out to editors. He was very good at his job, and I was lucky enough that he was able to provoke interest among several publishing houses." A reminiscent smile came over his face. I could tell he loved this part. "There was an auction. My first novel went for six figures, an enormous amount at the time, especially for an unknown name. But so much of it was timing. My first novel released about the same time as the first Jason Bourne movie with Matt Damon. Giles won the bidding war and became my editor. We turned out to be a wonderful team, the three of us. I wrote the books, Philip took care of the money and business, and Giles was in charge of editing and publishing. So long as he treated us well, which he was careful to do, everyone was happy."

"Until you died."

The reminiscent smile was replaced by his more recent petulant expression. "Must you keep bringing that up?"

"I'm sorry, but it is pretty relevant to the mess we're in right now."

He thumped his fist on his knee. "Candace Branson has a lot to answer for," he said in a furious undertone.

I was so glad he hadn't been the one to kill his ex-wife. What if he'd turned her into a vampire and I'd had to deal with an undead version of Candace Branson? It was bad enough having the constant bickering between Oscar Wilde and Bartholomew without adding in the bickering of two formerly married egomaniacs.

"She does. But we also need to figure out who killed her so we can get back to our regular, quiet lives."

He nodded. "And I can go out again with fewer restrictions."

I was pleased that there was a direct benefit to him in this. I needed his cooperation.

"So Bartholomew Branson is no longer an unknown name. Therefore, she might send the manuscript to several agents to get them competing for the chance to represent your next last book."

"Exactly. The woman's so grasping, I wouldn't be a bit surprised."

I looked around the room. "The two people who have the most to gain from Candace's death then, assuming she was killed because of the manuscript, are the two agents?"

Bartholomew looked miserable. "Not the American one. He'd already won the battle. Remember? You said he announced the morning after the launch that he was *my* new agent. He had no reason to kill Candace." He thumped the leather arm of the couch with his fist. "I can't believe that on top of hiring a ghost to write my books, she screwed over my agent. Does no one have loyalty anymore?"

I felt really sorry for him. "You know that this makes Philip Hazeltine the most likely suspect?"

"Not so fast," he said, and I could see his thriller mind spinning. "What if Giles were able to produce that manuscript and claim that I'd already sent it to him before I died? It's a twist in this plot we haven't explored."

I put a hand to my forehead. "But you just said the books went through Philip to Giles."

"No, no, no," he said, shaking his head as though I were being particularly clueless. "That was how the negotiations worked. But after seventeen novels, I no longer needed Philip's editorial advice. I would send the manuscripts straight to Giles."

"You mean he got them before Philip did?"

"Yes. Philip negotiated the contracts, but he'd ceased to be involved in the editorial process after about the third novel."

I was getting a really bad feeling in the pit of my stomach. "But if Giles claimed that you had sent him that manuscript, wouldn't Tristan Holt have something to say about it?" I had all their attention now.

Lochlan rose. "And didn't you say that Tristan was staying at O'Donnell House?"

"I did."

"Then he'll be your next victim," Bartholomew said. "It's the perfect turning point for act two."

"We've got to warn Tristan," I said. I liked the guy. I didn't want him to get killed over a manuscript that he hadn't even been properly paid for.

I was already reaching for my mobile phone when Lochlan stopped me. "Quinn, I have a better idea." We all looked at him. "What if we leave Tristan with his current plans? And when he's in bed asleep, whoever is willing to claim that Bartholomew sent them the manuscript will have to silence the true author."

"But he could get murdered, when we could stop it happening."

"He won't get murdered," Lochlan said, as though I were being silly. "One of us will be hidden in the wardrobe ready to catch the culprit red-handed."

"Not bad," Bartholomew said.

"I think I can improve on your plan," I said, warming to his idea. "What if it's not you hiding in the wardrobe but the Gardai?"

He nodded. I thought he was quite relieved not to have to

get more involved in police business than he already was. "Excellent idea, Quinn. But can you convince them?"

"If I get Tristan Holt's permission, then I think I can." I glanced at my watch. "But it's after seven o'clock now. There's no time to lose."

"He is rather putting himself at risk of being arrested himself, don't you think?" Lochlan asked. "He's got the best motive for murdering Candace Branson." Was he still trying to win the ten euros?

"I'm sure that the Gardai would rather catch the real culprit," I said.

"It all depends on whether you can get Tristan Holt to agree to be the cheese in our mousetrap."

ochlan said he'd take care of the Gardai. I knew he had connections in high places, so I left that part of the plan to him and said I'd see about getting Tristan on board.

I called Tristan on his pay-as-you-go mobile, grateful when he picked up. Surprisingly, when I explained the plan to him, Tristan seemed keen on the idea.

"Cool. I'll do it."

"You're sure? You know it's risky."

"I'm a writer, Quinn. This kind of firsthand research is too good to miss. And the cops will be hiding in the closet. I'll be fine."

To my surprise, I received a call from DI Walsh. "I understand we're doing a stakeout at the O'Donnell House," he said, sounding irked. He probably didn't like civilians getting involved in his business. "Tell me why I shouldn't arrest this Tristan Holt for the murder of Candace Branson? Sounds to me that he had the most to gain from her death."

I shook my head, even though he couldn't see me. "But he

didn't have much to gain. Without one of the key partners in Bartholomew Branson's publishing world, he's just another MFA trying to sell a book."

DI Walsh had been in the military and, in the ensuing silence, I suspected he was picturing maneuvers. Plotting out the capture of a murderer as though it were an enemy position. Finally, he said, "We'll have an officer inside that young man's room, and I'll post a couple outside. But Quinn, I warn you, if no one makes an attempt on Tristan Holt's life, it won't look good for him."

My heart began to pound. What had I done? Had I just put Tristan Holt, not so much in danger of his life from a murderer, but in danger of being arrested for a crime he hadn't committed? That was always assuming that he hadn't committed it. I didn't have anything other than my witch's intuition that he was innocent of Candace Branson's murder. However, we'd come this far now. We had to see it through.

Sneaking an officer into Tristan Holt's room turned out to be the most difficult part of the process. We had to enlist Karen's cooperation, and she came up with the genius idea of having someone disguise themselves as her staff.

"And Lord knows I need the help," she muttered. "I have a full house, and I could have as many rooms again rented out if I wanted, with all the media here and all. I only wish it was earlier in the day so she could clean the rooms while she's poking about."

DI Walsh suggested that the female detective could pretend to check the towels and turn down the beds, like in a posh hotel, which gave her a perfect excuse to check on everyone's whereabouts. Then she'd do Tristan Holt's room last, causing no suspicion when she entered his room, and who would notice that she never came out again? Besides, she could hide surveillance equipment in amongst the towels and things. I thought it was a brilliant plan.

Karen insisted I come over. "I haven't the right constitution for cloak and dagger. You must come and give me your support." In truth, I was excited to be part of this plot to catch a killer in the act. Well, not in the act, but close to it.

Tristan Holt seemed pretty excited when I got to O'Donnell House and explained I was there to visit Karen. He looked like a different man now that he was clean. He'd shaved, his hair was clean and combed and I suspected Karen had washed his clothes for him. The only moment of worry he showed was when he said, "Quinn, if this goes badly—" He didn't seem to know what to say next, so I assured him that everything would be fine.

"But if it does go wrong, make sure my book gets published, will you? If Bartholomew Branson can have a posthumous best-seller, maybe I can too. At least the money would help my mom."

It was so sweet, my heart warmed to him. I became doubly determined that nothing was going to happen to him. I said, "I have some protection amulets that a local witch gave me. It's very woo-woo here, being Ireland and all."

I gave him a leather band with a nice piece of black obsidian that he could wear around his wrist. It contained powerful protective magic, and then, when he was slipping it onto his wrist, I quietly recited a spell of protection.

I'd done all I could to keep him safe, but even so, I was as jumpy as Cerridwen when she's convinced there's a mouse behind the walls. He went back to the lounge where everyone was gathered while I sat with Karen in the kitchen. Except I couldn't stay seated or still. I kept pacing back and forth and couldn't even manage a sensible conversation.

"Quinn, you're making me more nervous than I was before you came."

"I feel responsible. I'm the one who talked both Tristan and the police into this crazy mousetrap of a scheme. What if it all goes wrong and Tristan Holt ends up dead?" Or if no one made an attempt on his life and DI Walsh decided that arresting a guy with a very strong motive who might be innocent was better than no arrest at all?

The constable arrived at the kitchen door, and I'd never have guessed she was a Garda if I hadn't already known it. She was in her thirties, with lank brown hair tied back in a ponytail. She wore jeans and a sweatshirt. She told us that she had backup in the garden, and DI Walsh slipped behind her into the kitchen. Karen gave her a basket with clean towels, and she slipped her surveillance gear into it before following Karen out into the dining room, which led to the hall and then the stairway to the rooms.

Karen came back and nodded to DI Walsh, who slipped back out into the back yard.

By ten, I could hear the B&B guests saying good night. I heard Tristan talking. He sounded more jovial than I'd ever heard him, which was strange seeing as he was about to offer himself up as bait to catch a killer. Then I heard the answering voice and recognized Chloe. Nice to know he might have spent the last night of his life hitting on a woman.

Karen made tea and put out a plate of homemade cookies. After my lean dinner of salmon, brown rice, and spinach, with not a bit of bread or butter or sauce, I was starving. I tucked into the cookies.

It was difficult to stay calm. At every creak of the old house, I wanted to jump out of my chair and run upstairs to make sure Tristan wasn't hurt. From the way she kept jumping in her chair every time a toilet flushed or the old house shifted, I suspected Karen felt the same way. She'd already lost one guest in her short stint of running this bed and breakfast. She really didn't need to lose another one.

By one, Karen was serving coffee to keep us both awake, and the cookie tin was empty.

By three in the morning, I thought I'd made a terrible mistake. Poor Tristan. What was I going to do if he got arrested?

I looked outside a few times. I didn't see any Gardai presence, but after a cloudy day, the sky was completely overcast. There wasn't a hint of moon or stars. It was *dark* dark. Still, once or twice, I thought I sensed movement rather than saw or heard anything outside. It could have been a cat or a fox or maybe even a badger.

By quarter to four, I was having trouble keeping my eyes open. I didn't know how cops did it. How could a stakeout be so tense and boring at the very same time?

Then I heard a crash that had us both jumping to our feet and shouting. Karen and I were on the move, nearly crashing into DI Walsh, who glared at me before sprinting up the stairs. We followed in hot pursuit and, when we got to the top of the stairs, saw an astonishing sight. Giles, wearing a dark red, silk dressing gown and slippers, was already handcuffed, and beside him, the constable who'd posed as a cleaning woman was holding on to his arm. The door to Tristan's room was standing wide open, and about three feet away, Philip Hazeltine stood stock still. He was at the other end of the hallway from his room and was wearing, like me, all black. Not night clothes either. He stood there as though if he was still enough, maybe no one would notice him and he could blend into the wallpaper. All the other doors were now open. Irving wore pajamas with cartoon rabbits on them.

"What's going on?" he asked, yawning hugely behind his hand.

Chloe's door opened last. She was so gorgeous, I seriously wondered if she wore makeup to bed.

The person I didn't see was Tristan Holt. I ran forward. "Tristan? Are you okay?"

He appeared behind the detective, who was still holding Giles by the arm.

"Yeah. I'm fine. That wasn't as exciting as I thought it would be."

I looked at him, and he was obviously whole and unharmed. "Did Giles try to kill you?"

"No. I don't know if he was going to, but he and Philip bumped into each other in the doorway to my room. It was more like the Keystone Cops than a murder."

"I can explain," Philip said, looking about as innocent as a guy standing over a corpse with a dagger dripping blood in his hand. Being dressed all in black really didn't help.

"So can I," Giles said, obviously trying to hold on to his dignity even though he was in handcuffs and the edge of his robe was slipping apart, revealing navy and maroon striped cotton pajamas. With his arms pulled back like that, one of his pajama buttons had popped open, revealing a sliver of his pale belly.

Suddenly, in this very awkward tableau, Karen Tate absolutely lost it. She said, "I am absolutely sick of this. I've barely opened my brand-new bed and breakfast, at great cost to myself, I might add, and I've got murderers and unwanted guests and police crawling all over the place at all hours of the day and night. I've had enough of all of you. I'm putting the coffee on, and I want every one of you in the front room and we'll hash this out now."

She was showing a side of herself I'd never seen. All of us jumped to attention, even Detective Inspector Walsh. After looking like he might argue with her, he suddenly nodded.

"Excellent idea, Ms. Tate."

"And if you've got any of those shortbread cookies, I'm kind of hungry. I was too nervous to eat dinner last night," Tristan said.

"Really."

He sent her a wheedling look. "I did nearly get murdered."

We all gathered downstairs in Karen Tate's front room. DI Walsh looked irritated, as though he'd lost a night's sleep for nothing, Philip and Giles both looked sheepish and embarrassed. Irving kept yawning, and Tristan was probably the one who looked wide awake. In fact, he looked wired. Chloe came in last, and she'd taken the time to dress in slim black trousers and a blue sweater, and she'd combed her hair. Weirdly, none of us talked about what was going on while Karen was slapping about in the kitchen. When the coffee was done, she called us all into the dining room, and we obediently sat around the big table. To Tristan's delight, she even slapped a plate of his favorite shortbreads in the middle of the table.

DI Walsh might be the top cop on the case, but this was

Karen's place, her business, and she was in a mood that brooked no-nonsense. It was actually really impressive.

"Now," she said, "before another day passes, I want to know exactly what's going on." She pointed her finger at Giles and said, "And I'll start with you."

The constable who'd been undercover in Tristan's wardrobe looked at DI Walsh with her eyebrows raised, but he shrugged. This might be unconventional, but Karen Tate might get more answers than anybody else. He seemed to think it was worth a try.

"Giles, I'm waiting to hear what you were doing entering Tristan Holt's room in the middle of the night."

The editor shifted uncomfortably in his seat as we all stared at him. "I wanted to talk to him, that's all."

DI Walsh interjected here, asking the constable, "Did you find a weapon on him?"

She shook her head. "Nothing."

"But then Candace Branson's murderer didn't need any other weapon than his bare hands," DI Walsh said in a conversational tone. "Is that what you were going to do? Strangle Tristan Holt the way you strangled Candace Branson?"

Giles visibly recoiled from the suggestion. "I can't imagine why you'd even think such a thing."

"Then if you didn't go into Tristan Holt's room at four in the morning to kill him, why did you go in?"

"I told you. I wanted to talk to him."

"And it couldn't wait until morning?"

"No. It couldn't."

"What did you want to talk to him about?"

The editor looked rather shiftily around the table. "I'd rather speak to him in private."

"Unless you want to talk down at the station, I suggest you speak up now."

"It's very awkward." And then he looked down at himself. "And I'm not even dressed."

Even though it was serious, I had to press my lips together to stop from smiling. I wasn't sure if he was more upset about being accused of murder or being caught in his pajamas in the middle of the night.

"Oh, very well. I wanted to speak to Tristan about working with me."

"Why, you double-crossing—"

"Irving, please. Let the man speak," Karen Tate said, quelling him with a glance.

"I had a feeling that Tristan might be the real author of the supposedly newly discovered Bartholomew Branson manuscript," Giles said.

"That's rather a stretch, isn't it?" DI Walsh asked. "What made you think that?"

Giles looked more and more uncomfortable. They'd removed his handcuffs so he looked less like a felon. He sipped his coffee for something to do, or probably to buy time, and then slumped back in his chair. "I knew when Candace Branson made her announcement that Bartholomew Branson could not have written that manuscript. You see, he talked over every new book with me. He'd already emailed me a rough sketch of the new book before his unfortunate demise. There was absolutely no reason why Candace Branson would ever have known anything about it. They weren't on terms."

"Doesn't mean—"

"Irving," Karen said, with her finger raised. "I'm not telling you again."

"I'd managed to catch a glimpse of the manuscript, and I have to say it was good." He glanced over at Tristan now, who was watching with rapt attention, a half-eaten cookie forgotten in his hand. "Very good. You're a talented author and quite gifted at recreating Bartholomew Branson's style."

"Thanks," Tristan said. "That means a lot."

Karen Tate said, "I wouldn't get too excited. Nobody's convinced that Giles wasn't going in your room to strangle you."

Giles looked truly confused. "Why on earth would I kill the golden goose?"

"Or silence the goose."

DI Walsh turned to Philip then. "And what were you doing? Also trying to gain entry into Tristan Holt's room?"

"I also had something to discuss with him," Philip said, trying to sound dignified.

DI Walsh said, "And there you were, all dressed in black. Ready to leave at a moment's notice. I happened to look in your room and noticed that your bags are all packed. Planning a quick exit, were you?"

The agent grew red in the face. "Yes, as a matter of fact, I was leaving. But I had no intention of killing that young man," he said, nodding in the direction of Tristan.

"Thanks, man."

"Like Giles here, I also wanted to talk to him. I-I may have overheard some of the conversation between Tristan and Candace at the party at Devil's Keep so I already knew he was the author. I was only going to tell him that I had to leave early to get back to Dublin. A water pipe burst in my house. My wife needs me home. I was going to invite him to come to the office when he was finished here and we'd talk about his future."

For somebody who'd gone to bed being afraid he'd be murdered, Tristan Holt's night was turning out a lot better than could have been expected. "Really? You want to talk to me? You mean, like, about representation?"

"Yes."

My phone buzzed with a text. There was only one person I could think of who'd be texting at this time of the night, so I quietly checked the message.

And then I knew who had killed Candace Branson.

CHAPTER 20

There was an odd silence, as no one seemed to know what to say or do next. It built for a beat or two, and then I said, "Irving, you're an agent. How come you didn't go barging into Tristan Holt's room in the middle of the night like the rest of them?"

He looked quite surprised to be questioned. He'd been sitting there with that pouting scowl on his face and jerked to attention at my words. "Why would I? I'm not some sneaking Brit. Plus, I already have the contract, don't forget."

Philip pretty much jeered at him. "A contract that will be null and void since the person you made it with is deceased. Any contract needs to be made with the author of the book."

Irving leaned forward and jabbed his finger towards Philip. "When my lawyers are finished with you, you'll be mincemeat. And destitute. Destitute mincemeat. Sounds like something you limeys would eat."

"Where is this contract?" I asked him.

He turned to me, looking confused. "What?"

"The contract you had with Candace Branson. I'm sure Detective Inspector Walsh would like to see it."

The DI looked as though that had been the last thing he'd been thinking of, but with a quick glance at me, he said, "Yes. We will need to see that. It's evidence."

Irving got huffy. "It's my proprietary business information."

The DI looked like he was getting fed up with this. "As I said before, you'd be most welcome to come down to the station if you'd prefer to continue our discussions there."

Irving puffed his chest out and looked even more belligerent. "Fine. I don't carry those things around. The contract's in my office back in New York."

"I'm sure your assistant could email it," I said.

He sent me a nasty look. "You're a clerk in a bookstore. What do you know?"

While that was true, it was pretty rude of him to say it in that condescending manner. And it was exactly the opening I needed. "I manage that bookshop and, as you may have noticed from the gala opening party, I'm pretty well-connected in publishing."

This was completely untrue, but Irving didn't know that I'd had the combined resources of Bartholomew Branson and Lochlan Balfour at my disposal. It was obvious that whoever had organized that gala did have excellent connections in publishing. It was sort of embarrassing that I'd gotten all the credit, but right now that was paying off. I said, "You don't have a contract at all."

He stood up so fast, he knocked his chair over. "You don't know what you're talking about. Course I do, and if Candace Branson was here, she'd set you straight."

"But she's not here, is she?" I shook my head. "Everyone I've spoken to remarked on how important money was to Candace Branson. When she was married to Bartholomew, I understand she was always asking for bigger advances. Money was far more important to Candace than loyalty. Right, Philip?"

"Yes, indeed. Not that I wish to speak ill of the dead."

"So I started thinking. If she was willing to abandon both the editor and the agent that Bartholomew Branson had worked with for his whole career in order to sign with you, then what was to stop her aiming even higher?"

Irving jammed a sausage-like finger at my face. "Because we had a deal."

"Now that's a funny thing. Because Mr. Myron Warner also seems to think he has a deal with Candace Branson for *All Fall Down*. And he did email me his contract." He hadn't, his assistant had emailed it to Lochlan, but that was a detail that would only muddy the waters.

Beneath his belligerent attitude, I could see Irving was shaken when I uttered that name.

"You see, I do have connections in publishing. She'd been after him for years, hadn't she? Myron Warner is the agent who is famous for blockbuster movie deals, getting top dollar for his authors, and dropping them the minute they aren't selling. It's probably why Bartholomew never wanted to sign with him. But Candace did. Giles heard an American man arguing with Candace that night. We all thought it was Tristan. But it wasn't, was it? It was you."

"That's ridiculous." He tried to sound tough, but I could see the sweat glistening on his forehead. "And so what? If Candy wanted to go to a different agent, I wasn't going to stop her. Sure, a new Branson novel would be something, but I have a huge list of clients. I didn't need it."

"That's not what my sources in New York tell me. You were betting everything on this new book. Things haven't been going so well for you lately, have they?"

"Never better." He blinked as a drop of sweat landed in his eye.

I shook my head. "My sources in New York tell me that your agency's in big trouble financially. You needed this sure-fire hit. You're losing your big clients, you're deep in debt, and a brand-new Bartholomew Branson was going to change all of that. You even came all the way to a tiny, little town in Ireland so you could stay close to Candy. And then she ripped the rug right out from under you."

"That's nothing but a bunch of circumstantial evidence. It won't hold up in court. And I'm an American. I have rights."

DI Walsh interjected again. "So did Candace Branson. She had the right to justice. Sure, the evidence is circumstantial, but if Quinn's right, it's substantial. And certainly gives us reasonable cause to investigate you and your business." That boxer's face cracked in a grin. "Like Quinn here, I have sources in New York. Friends in the FBI."

"It was Myron Warner who called Candace at two in the morning. He forgot about the time difference calling from New York. You knew your business was finished. You were finished. So, you killed her and took her cell phone. What did you do with it? Bury it in the back garden? Sneak to the ocean and toss it in? Doesn't matter. Myron Warner will testify that he called her and that he had a contract with Candace Branson. It's over, Irving."

Irving then did a very stupid thing. He panicked and tried

to run. He pushed away from the table and sprinted for the front door. I had no idea how far he thought he'd get, but he obviously hadn't counted on running right into the arms of the Gardai in Karen's front garden.

When Sergeant Kelly, who'd been in the garden, had read Irving his rights and escorted him out of the bed and breakfast, there was definitely a sense of anticlimax. It was too late to go to bed and too early to do much of anything else. Karen looked around the table at us and shrugged helplessly.

"Shall I put on some breakfast?"

Weirdly, I was starving. I think a wakeful night of stress and worry were to blame. Giles and Philip looked at each other and said in unison, "Why not?"

Tristan rubbed his very flat stomach. "I haven't been able to eat properly in days. I could murder a full Irish."

"You want some help?" I asked. It didn't seem fair that Karen should be stuck doing the breakfast for all of us, but she shook her head. She looked happier than she had before the murder.

"Quinn, I need the activity. It'll calm me down. I've been utterly stressed for days now. And finally, it's over. I have my home and my business back."

She nearly danced back into the direction of the kitchen.

Tristan looked down at the table. "I feel awful that I contributed to her stress."

"Well, make sure you leave her a nice tip," I said. It was a hint to everybody around the table. "And an excellent review on Tripadvisor."

There was enthusiastic nodding. "I shall tell all my friends about this place," Giles said. "I believe we could put your little town on the map, Quinn. With your charming bookshop and your publishing contacts, Ballydehag could be a veritable Hay-on-Wye."

"I have no idea what that is," I said. Hay-on-Wye? It sounded like a farmer's field going through an identity crisis.

They both chuckled in that superior British manner. "Hay-on-Wye is a small, out-of-the-way town on the border of Wales. For some unknown reason, it's got some of the best bookshops in the world and runs a world-famous literary festival."

"Really? I'll have to check it out."

"You should. I could see you doing something similar here. Of course, you'll need more accommodation, but I believe that between us, Philip and I could bring in some first-rate authors for you."

I was growing quite excited at this idea. Now that I knew that we could put on a great event, especially if Lochlan got involved and, even better, if he opened the castle to gala events, people would come from far and wide.

"Maybe we could even get people who live around here with an extra room or two to offer guest accommodation." I started to laugh. "We could call it Book and Breakfast."

"I like the way you think. We must definitely begin planning this."

Then Giles turned to Tristan and looked quite stern. "And as for you, young man."

Tristan stopped him with his two hands up in the air, as though he were surrendering to somebody who was pointing a gun at him. "I know. I'm sorry. I don't know what to say. It started innocently enough. I entered a contest. How was I supposed to know it would turn into a famous author's widow trying to scam him?"

Giles nodded. "Fair point. Do you have a copy of that manuscript you wrote? I managed to catch a peek at it during the gala, but I only snatched a glimpse."

The author looked miserable. "On my laptop. At home. I could email it to you."

I was a big believer in the old strike-while-the-iron-is-hot philosophy of life and work. I said, "I have a copy."

And I reached into my bag and pulled out the now slightly tattered printout. To my amusement, both Giles and Philip reached for the manuscript at the same time.

Giles chuckled. "This is awkward."

Feeling very much like Solomon pulling babies apart, I handed Giles the first half of the manuscript and Philip the second. When he raised his eyebrows at me, I said, "You'll get an idea of his writing style. And you two can swap halves afterward."

"Unorthodox, but all right." And, reaching into his pocket, he brought out his reading glasses. No doubt when he'd been sneaking into Tristan's room, he'd been hoping for a peek at that manuscript all along.

Both men began to read quietly. Once Philip said, "Um pum," and tapped his manicured finger in the middle of the page.

Giles said, "Does anyone have a pen?"

There was one by the guestbook on the buffet, and I reached over and passed it to him. He made a note in the margin.

I glanced at Tristan, who was biting his nails watching the

two men with something between fear and hope. When Giles made another note in the manuscript's margin, Tristan jumped up and said, "I can't stand this." He walked to the window and stared out into the garden.

I completely felt for him. My stomach was clenched partly in dread and partly in anticipation. I couldn't imagine what it was like to be the actual author, watching two giants in publishing read his unpublished manuscript. Poor guy.

Philip said, "Um pum," one more time, and Tristan moved away from the window.

In a desperate under-voice, he said to me, "I'm going to go help Karen in the kitchen. I'll have a heart attack if I stand here listening to those two much longer."

I nodded and whispered back, "I'll call you if you're needed."

I didn't think either the agent or the editor even noticed the poor author had scampered away like a frightened rabbit. What I noticed was they both kept reading. I was no expert, but I suspected that if the editor was already making notes in the margin and crossing out the odd word to suggest a better one, that that had to be a very good sign.

After about ten minutes, Giles had a small stack of pages beside him and was continuing to read. Philip looked up and said, "Mind if I have a glance at the beginning?"

Giles looked up at him as though he'd forgotten he was there. "What's that?"

"Can I look at the beginning, please?"

"Oh, yes, help yourself."

Philip reached for the pages, and once more they both settled into reading. It didn't take Philip long to get through those five pages, since he wasn't making notes. After he'd finished them, he sat back, regarding the pages in front of him with a pensive look on his face. What did that mean? Did he not want to read anymore because he was bored? Because he'd already decided that Tristan Holt was just one of a million aspiring authors? Giles read on for another page or two and then glanced up to find Philip staring at him. He gave a small, slightly superior smile. "What do you think?"

I felt almost embarrassed to be there, like they were discussing their bank balances or something and had forgotten I was present. But I was dying to know what they had to say, so I kept quiet and still and tried to act like a piece of furniture.

Philip said, "I rather think I may have found myself a new client."

Giles nodded and looked pleased. "And I'd be very happy to take a look at anything you might care to submit on his behalf."

Then they looked around and seemed surprised to find Tristan's chair empty. I said, "You should call him in. The poor guy was having a heart attack watching you guys read his work."

They both chuckled as though handling nervous authors was a daily occurrence. Giles began to rise, and Philip said, "No. I'll go."

He went off in the direction of the kitchen and very soon returned with a beaming Tristan. Tristan looked at me and said, "I can't believe it. Philip Hazeltine wants to represent me."

I was almost as excited as he was. "That's great. And the next time you launch a book, I hope you'll consider The Blarney Tome."

He laughed delightedly. "I wouldn't have my Irish launch anywhere else."

Giles rose, not to be left out of this little scene. He went forward and offered his hand to shake. "And, pending me giving your entire manuscript a proper read, I believe I can welcome you to my publishing house. I take on very few new authors, but I'd be prepared to make an exception in your case."

Tristan grabbed for his hand rather in the manner of a seal jumping in the air for a fish. Philip said, "Let's not be hasty, Tristan. I believe your manuscript will garner quite a bit of interest in publishing circles. The very reason you have an agent is to make sure you don't take the first offer. Besides, in order to put the Bartholomew Branson name onto a new novel, we'd need the permission of the heir to Mr. Branson's literary estate."

Giles's gaze sharpened. "Do you know who that is, now that Candace is gone?"

Philip's smile was very superior, but he addressed his words to Tristan Holt rather than to Giles. "The estate passes to a niece, I understand. One of the benefits of signing with me is you'll find I'm very thorough. I have already sent a letter to the niece expressing my condolences and offering to explain the terms of the will and how best to handle the very lucrative inheritance."

Giles looked quite offended. "With you remaining on as the agent of record, of course. Now come on, old man. You and I have worked on Bartholomew Branson's manuscripts for his entire career. Once you have the legalities worked out, naturally we want to continue publishing any books that continue the series."

Philip said, "And I'm sure my client and I would be happy to consider your publishing house. But we'll expect a generous advance."

Giles' mouth opened and closed a few times. "But he can't expect the same advance Bartholomew Branson was getting. That would be preposterous."

"Money isn't the only factor. I'm going to counsel my client that he should have his name on any future Barthomew Branson book as co-author."

Giles gave it some thought and then nodded. "I think that's a very good idea. Especially if you've got more novels in you. Have you, Mr. Holt?"

I was impressed that Tristan had moved up in the world from "young man" to "Mr. Holt." Philip was already starting to earn his commission.

"I can write as many books in the style of Bartholomew Branson as you can publish. But I'd also like to talk to you about my own work."

CHAPTER 21

When Karen Tate came in with a heaping tray of food, the three men were deeply engaged in planning out Tristan Holt's budding career.

As I helped Karen set the plates of food out and bring in more coffee, she said, "Is it going well for Tristan, then?"

"I think so. And I believe we've just found you a whole load of extra business. What if we had a yearly book festival here? And you were in charge of accommodations?"

I told her my idea about getting people in the village to offer extra rooms. She got quite excited at the idea and agreed that she would head any committee we set up for the purpose.

Breakfast was a much happier affair than I could have imagined. Tristan was about to see his wildest dreams come true, and Philip and Giles were obviously expecting a profitable partnership with a new author.

Over his second cup of coffee, Giles said, "I mean no disrespect to the dead, but Tristan has a better command of prose than poor Bartholomew ever did."

"Agreed," Philip said. "But the books still need to be true to the brand. It was Bartholomew's preposterous plots that people loved so much."

I was having an idea. I said, "I'm kind of an expert on Bartholomew Branson myself. Tristan, if you want, I could take a look at your manuscripts too and offer suggestions. If it would be helpful."

Agent and editor looked at me slightly askance, but Tristan looked beyond thrilled at the idea. "I know. You're a total expert. I remember the way you quizzed me on the books. It would be great to have the feedback of a genuine fan."

"Great," I said brightly. "Why don't I take this manuscript back again, and you can email these two clean copies."

I could tell that neither Philip nor Giles wanted to let that manuscript out of their sights, but it was Tristan's manuscript, after all. They begrudgingly agreed to give it up to me when Tristan had promised them he'd email them a fresh copy. I could have told them I already had a full manuscript at my cottage, but that would involve explaining that I'd ended up with Candace's. In all the excitement of murder and mayhem, no one had questioned where Candace's manuscript had gone. I was happy to leave it that way.

Besides, I was beginning to see how important it was to tantalize these two. If they had to wait a day or two for Tristan to email them his book, I was certain they'd survive.

I went home full to bursting from Karen's amazing breakfast, the manuscript safely in my possession. I asked Dierdre to open the shop for me because all I could think about was getting into my bed and sleeping for several hours. I texted

Lochlan to let him know how everything had gone and suggested a vampire book club meeting that night so I could tell everybody the good news.

Especially Bartholomew.

I'd have called him directly, but I wasn't sure how well he'd take the news that Philip and Giles had so easily found his replacement. I thought it would be better delivered in the company of other vampires who could control him if he had another temper tantrum.

I was so sleepy when I got back to the cottage that I didn't notice the obvious clues that should have alerted me there was trouble in the house.

Cerridwen was nowhere to be seen. That wasn't like her. Since I'd been out all night, I'd expected her to greet me at the door. I hoped I'd find her sleeping upstairs on the bed, but as I got to the bottom of the staircase, I could hear voices. And the television was playing.

I was tired, cranky, and I had a lot of leftover adrenaline to deal with from a stressful night in which I'd worried that a man I'd set up as bait in a trap might have ended up dead. So I was in no mood for Biddy O'Donnell and her tricks. I stomped up the stairs and burst into my bedroom. I was accustomed to finding Biddy making herself at home on my bed, her nasty familiar curled up by her side, but even so, the sight that met my eyes shocked me.

She wasn't alone on the bed. Pyewacket stared at me balefully, her body curled up between Biddy and the seventeenth-century reprobate Thomas Blood. They made a very peculiar pair, Biddy with her cap and dingy gown, smelling like a woman who'd been underground for several hundred years, and Thomas Blood in his bright red jacket with the brass buttons, his long, flowing curls, frilled shirt and breeches. I was annoyed to see he hadn't even bothered to take off his leather boots before settling himself on my bed. They didn't even notice me, they were so busy watching the *Antiques Roadshow.*

"Would you look at that," Thomas Blood said. "Zounds, I swear those are oak panels from a church that somebody's cut out and stuck in the back of a settle."

"I do believe you're right," Biddy said.

I looked at the screen and saw a very old-looking bench with panels that were set into it that did indeed look like something out of a church.

"I'm sure there were screens carved like that in my parish of—"

"Shhh," Biddy said, putting her hand over his mouth. "Let's see if he gets it right this time."

Gleefully they listened as the furniture expert told a very posh-looking woman that the bench she had inherited was not from the Renaissance period, but that several original panels from a church or cathedral had been repurposed into the back of the bench and they were from the Renaissance.

"Still, it's a very nice piece. At auction it would probably fetch about seven to eight hundred pounds."

"Seven hundred pounds," Thomas Blood burst out, pushing Biddy's hand off his mouth. "Seven hundred pounds for a hodgepodge of an old bench?"

"That's what I'm telling you, Thomas. There's good money to be made in flogging off a load of people's old junk."

I couldn't stand here any longer and listen to them. "What do you two think you're doing?" I asked in my firmest voice.

They both turned to stare at me. "What are you doing home? You're supposed to be at the shop." Biddy glared at me as though I were the one in the wrong.

"I didn't get any sleep all night, and I came home to have a nap. Which is difficult to do with you two, and your cat, in my bed."

"Well, where else are we to go? You've warned me off my own ancestral home," Biddy said, as though she had any right to be in Karen's place.

"And we're going into business together," Thomas Blood said with a flourish, as though that made it all right for me to give up my bed.

"You're going into business together? Doing what?"

The thought of those two in some kind of shop, with their peculiar garb and ancient speech patterns, was almost too much. Luckily, I knew that the other vampires would put a stop to it. Still, those two doing anything together was slightly alarming, as Pyewacket probably had better standards of right and wrong than those two.

"It's the eBay," Biddy said.

"Aye, the eBay," Thomas Blood said as though he had any idea what it even was.

"What are you two planning to do with *the* eBay?" I asked them, crossing my arms over my chest and looking down at them.

"I've set up my own shop. Biddy's Antiques." She looked over graciously at Thomas Blood and said, "Though we could change it to Biddy and Blood."

"That's got a really nice ring to it," I said.

"No, no," Thomas said. "I'm happy to be more of a silent partner."

Considering the man had tried to steal the Crown Jewels, I thought he was very smart to stay out of the limelight, even hundreds of years later. Somebody might recognize him from a history book.

"You're going to sell antiques on eBay?"

"Aye. You'd be surprised how many people do it, and all over the world too."

"Biddy, you need an internet address."

She looked very shifty here. "I know."

"Biddy. What have you done?"

I could see she was looking over at my laptop, which I'd left on my dressing table this morning.

I shook my head. "Don't you even think about using my internet."

"Well, then, you'll have to help me get my own. And you're going to have to get faster broadband."

I couldn't believe I was being chastised for not having good enough internet by an ancient witch.

"There's excellent internet at the castle," Thomas Blood said. "I may not like the place—it's more of a dungeon and a prison than a home—but Lochlan Balfour does not stint on the internet, I'll give you that."

"That's an excellent idea," I said, smiling for the first time since I'd arrived in my own cottage. "I think you should go over right now and talk to Lochlan about setting you up in business. He's an internet billionaire. Nobody could be a better business mentor for you than he."

Biddy looked at me like this might be a trick. But the only trick I had in mind was getting that old witch out of my bed and her smelly cat and her boot-wearing beau along with her.

"But if I don't like it, I'll be back."

"Oh, you'll like it," I promised.

I waited until the three of them had left and then called Lochlan. Rapidly, I explained what I'd done, and I was happy to see he was more amused than annoyed.

"The two of them are going to run an online antiques business?"

"Actually, I think it's a really good idea. It'll keep them both out of trouble and stop Thomas Blood from creating mayhem. He does it because he's so bored."

"There is something in what you're saying."

"I was hoping you would agree. But you have to do me a big favor."

"Taking that ancient, old crone and her familiar off your hands isn't a big enough favor?"

I rolled my eyes. "Another favor." I didn't quite know how to put this. "I need you to tell Biddy that you won't set her up with her internet business until she removes the spell from the O'Donnell House. From now on, all the televisions have to play all the stations and all the television programs that are available and not exclusively *Antiques Roadshow*."

"I'll do it, Quinn." There was a pause, and he said, "You don't think you should send her back where she came from, do you?"

"Only every day. But something always stops me. I think she may be an old reprobate, but she's my million-times-great-grandmother. And maybe if I'm lenient with her, some other witch will one day be lenient with me."

"I'll do as you ask. But, be warned, I will be keeping my eye on both of them."

"I heartily hope you do."

AFTER A LONG SLEEP, I felt much more refreshed. Even better, that afternoon, Karen Tate called me, excitement brimming over in her voice.

"You won't believe it, Quinn. That glitch in my electric system seems to have sorted itself out. The television is playing all kinds of different programs."

"That's great, but how come I can hear the intro to *Antiques Roadshow* playing in the background?"

She laughed. "That's Giles and Philip in the front room. They've become hooked on it."

I laughed too. "At least it's keeping them happy and out of trouble."

"I've never seen two men so happy. And they've both written me glowing reviews for the bed and breakfast. And so has Tristan. And I'm fully booked for the next two weeks."

Even though she couldn't see me, I punched the air with my fist. "That's great, Karen."

"And you know those scales that went missing?"

"Yes." I hoped she wasn't about to tell me that she'd found them on BiddyandBlood.com.

"I found them. I must have accidentally put them inside a cupboard when I thought I'd put them in the display cabinet. I'm so relieved. In fact, all the little bits and bobs I thought were missing have turned up."

"I'm so glad." I'd forgotten to tell Biddy she had to put everything she'd stolen back. Lochlan must have thought of that on his own.

With the O'Donnell House back to normal and Biddy and

Thomas Blood hopefully too busy to cause any more trouble, I only had one more thing to worry about.

Somebody was going to have to tell Bartholomew Branson that his publisher had found a new Bartholomew within only a couple of months of his death. No one liked to be replaceable, especially not someone with an ego like his.

It was nice to spend the afternoon in my shop, putting everything back the way I liked it.

Karen and I met for a celebration dinner in the pub, where we toasted her new success and started throwing out ideas for a literary festival the following year.

I went back to the shop to set up for the book club. Lochlan arrived early, looking casually elegant in jeans and a black sweater. With a flourish, he handed me a ten euro note. "Your winnings, and may I say I've rarely been happier to lose a wager."

I accepted the money saying, "I know. Tristan's a really nice guy. I'm so glad he didn't end up charged with a crime he didn't commit."

"Even better, it seems he's profiting from Bartholomew and Candace Branson's deaths without having to cause them."

"Good thing you have such great connections or Irving might have got away with murder."

"Yes. And you have good instincts. It was easy enough to find out who the biggest celebrity literary agents were and discover which one Candace had signed with."

"Behind Irving's back. And, speaking of sneaking around people's backs, you must have some extremely good sources to find out so quickly that Irving was nearly bankrupt."

He looked down at me, his blue eyes glittering. "When you've been around as long as I have, you develop extremely good networks."

By ten o'clock, everyone was assembled, and we even had a guest. Thomas had dragged Biddy along with him, saying there was a lot of value in old books. And besides, he was teaching her to read.

She wasn't a vampire, however. Lochlan looked at me, and I shrugged. It was his club, not mine. He said, "Very well, but you're on probation, Mistress O'Donnell."

She snorted. "And so are you, young gentleman. I don't normally mix with your kind. It's only that I'm a poor, old witch, made homeless by my own kin, that I've had to seek a home in a castle of the undead."

Before I could launch into the hot speech that was bursting to come out of my mouth, Lochlan put up a finger. "We all know that if it weren't for your many times great-granddaughter Quinn here, you'd be living in an underground prison. I offer you my castle as a refuge and a place to run your business, but I'm watching you. If there's any trouble at the castle, or at O'Donnell House, or at Quinn's cottage or place of business, I will take whatever action I believe appropriate."

Her cunning eyes darted everywhere, but it was pretty clear everyone was in agreement with Lochlan. She tried to look pitiful and failed and then said, "Fine. I've a business to run and no time to be traipsing about anyway."

"Good. And while you're out searching for antiques, I have a commission for you. I'd be interested if you find any old tapestries in good condition. Particularly Flemish ones. I think they'd spruce up the castle to no end."

Her eyes lit up. "Naturally, we'd expect a finder's fee."

Lochlan looked down his aristocratic Viking's nose at her. "Naturally."

"And no fakes," I put in. "They'd better be original, and they'd better not be stolen. I'll be getting a tapestry expert to evaluate them." We all knew such people existed because we'd been watching *Antiques Roadshow.*

"Fine," she snapped.

"And, now you mention it, if you happen to come across any interesting old books, especially first editions, bring them to me so I have first refusal." Maybe this antique gig wasn't going to be such a bad idea after all.

"Since the mistress cannot read," Thomas Blood said, "I will engage myself to search out such books and manuscripts that might be of interest to you, Mistress Callahan."

"Thank you, Thomas."

"That's great. Everybody's getting what they want except for me," Bartholomew Branson said. He looked particularly sorry for himself, slouched in a chair off to the side.

I glanced at Lochlan, and he nodded slightly, silently telling me to go on. "About that. I found the manuscript that your ex-wife was trying to pass off as yours."

He perked up at that and sat up straighter in his chair. "Really? Who was the writer? Some unsuccessful competitor, no doubt."

"No. It's a brand-new author. If you're interested, I happen to have a copy of the manuscript right here."

"You bet I'm interested." He stood up and came forward with his hand out. I handed him the manuscript and mentally crossed my fingers that he wouldn't turn into a raving madman when he read it.

We all watched as he began to read. Slowly, his expression changed from one of distaste to concentration. He read two pages and then flipped forward a few pages and skimmed. He glanced up at me. "This isn't too shabby. He's not up to my standard yet, of course, but it sounds like me. He's been respectful, what I would call 'in the style of' rather than a direct copy."

"I'm so relieved you think so. Since the author in question falsely believes that I am an expert on your books, he's agreed to let me read them before they get published."

"But Quinn, that's a brilliant plan. And you, of course, will pass the manuscripts on to me so I can make suggestions and help this poor, young writer to perfect his craft."

I was so pleased he saw it that way. "Exactly. It'll keep your brand pure."

"Won't bring you in any lovely money, though," Oscar Wilde reminded us all.

Bartholomew shook his head. "No. And I do need money. But, fortunately, I'm writing a new series of my own. I shall begin again," he said with a dramatic flourish. "Reinvent myself. I'll send the books to agents under a nom de plume. I'm sure I'll be snapped up."

"Actually, that's not a bad idea," I said. I hoped very much that he would become as much of a success in his second career as he had been in his first, but at least the undead author looked much happier than he had in the past few weeks. He had a purpose now.

I explained to him that they were going to put Tristan Holt's name on the books along with his, and he nodded enthusiastically. "Good. Don't want that young fellow passing off his beginner prose as mine." Then he looked quite concerned. "But his name will be in much smaller letters than mine, won't it?"

"Oh, yes. It's your name that will sell the books."

"Good. And then I'll have my second writing name to earn me all the money I need."

There was a sound like a moan that came from Oscar Wilde's direction. "Dear Bartholomew, I offer you half my prodigious fortune if you promise never to write another word."

Before a brawl could break out, I said, "And now, who's read this week's book? *The Body in the Library* by Agatha Christie?"

Thanks for reading *A Spelling Mistake!* I hope you enjoyed Quinn's adventure. Keep reading for a sneak peek of the next mystery, *A Poisonous Review,* Vampire Book Club Book 4.

A Poisonous Review , Chapter 1

"Have you heard the news, Quinn?" Kathleen McGinnis asked with eyes so bright and full of suppressed excitement that I knew she'd be devastated if I'd already heard whatever she wanted to tell me.

I stopped unpacking the new order of books that had just arrived at The Blarney Tome in Ballydehag, Ireland, where I currently managed the only bookshop in the village.

Before I could ask what the news was, my door opened again.

The second visitor was Karen Tate, another shop owner in town. "Have you heard?" she asked, her expression eager.

Kathleen owned Finnegan's, the local grocery store, and Karen was the proprietor of Granny's Drawers, which sold everything from old clothes and junk to antiques. She also ran Ballydehag's only bed and breakfast. Karen was actually a cousin of mine, but I couldn't tell her that for many reasons.

"What's the news?" I asked.

In a town the size of Ballydehag it doesn't take a lot to get everybody excited. No doubt somebody was getting married, or having a baby, or had been seen in a nearby town with someone they shouldn't be with. I liked gossip as much as the next person, so I waited in anticipation.

"The bakery's finally been rented!" Kathleen said and then settled back to see the result of her revelation.

Karen nodded. "Can you believe it, Quinn? Finally, the bakery's been rented."

Honestly, not since 'Netherfield's been let,' had words sounded so full of import.

"That's great," I said, trying to sound sufficiently excited. In fact, it would be very nice to get some good, freshly-baked bread again.

Kathleen did her best bringing in the kind of bread already packaged in bags that every grocery store has, but the bakery that had been operating when I'd first arrived in Ballydehag had produced outstanding loaves, and we hadn't had any since it closed under very unfortunate circumstances. I supposed not a lot of bakers wanted to ply their trade in a town as small as ours. There wasn't a lot of scope for expansion. Still, if you wanted a nice quiet life in a pretty and very traditional Irish village, you could do a lot worse. I hoped the new baker wouldn't be too sensitive to things like witches wandering the main street or vampires living in the local castle. So long as they were sufficiently oblivious to the supernatural, the new people could be very happy here.

"Don't you want to know who's rented it?" Kathleen asked.

"You're obviously dying to tell me, and I have no objection to hearing it," I replied. I really had to stop doing this, as now I was channeling Austen. Still, I couldn't help but hope that the bakery would be taken over by a handsome bachelor. Though with my luck, he'd be a Wickham, not a Darcy. Maybe I should concentrate on being grateful for fresh bread.

"Well, his name is Paddy McGrath. I only saw him out the window. A nicely dressed gentleman, wearing a proper jacket and tie. Seemed very pleasant."

"Is he single?" Karen asked.

She and I were two of the only middle-aged, single women in town and, frankly, the pickings were slim. Apart from Dr. Andrew Milsom, who I suspected had come here to get away from a woman, though he said it was to enjoy the fishing, there weren't many appropriate unattached men. Of course, most of my social life, if you could call it that, came from my undead book club. Since I was a witch myself, I was perfectly happy to mingle with other supernatural creatures, though they weren't without their challenges.

I wasn't as blatantly curious as Karen, but I was certainly interested in the answer. Was this Paddy McGrath unmarried? It would certainly be nice to have more single men in the community. It would be nice, for instance, to be able to go out for dinner with one. Vampires make very poor dining companions.

"I couldn't say. Bakeries are usually run by families, though, aren't they?" Kathleen shrugged, then said somewhat regretfully, "Besides, he wasn't very tall. Pleasant of countenance, but a little lacking in the height department."

Karen and I glanced at each other, but neither of us said anything. We'd have to make our own evaluations of Mr. Paddy McGrath.

Karen said, "Shall we go to the pub for dinner tonight to celebrate?"

I thought this was taking things a bit far. "You want to celebrate that somebody's taking over the bakery?"

"No, silly. It's Friday. We usually celebrate the end of the week."

This was true. We often had dinner together at the pub on Friday night. I don't know that we were celebrating the end of the week, since both of us had our shops open on Saturdays, but it had become a pleasant routine. I nodded and turned to Kathleen. "Would you care to join us?"

"Well, I won't stay for dinner, but I'd be happy to join you in a drink." That sounded perfect. Kathleen held my gaze. "And we're still on for the foraging tomorrow?"

I was surprised she'd mentioned it in front of Karen. Kathleen had promised to show me some of the more interesting herbs and even some mushrooms that would be useful in my spells and tonics. I had come from Seattle where the climate was similar but not exactly the same. Things like soil and the kinds of trees and weather always affected how things grew. I knew there were plants growing here that I had no knowledge of.

Kathleen, a pretty good witch herself, would be a good teacher. But Karen wasn't a witch. If she came along, what were we going to do? Harvest edible mushrooms?

Fortunately, Karen shook her head with a laugh. "I can't imagine anything worse than digging in the dirt on my hands and knees. Besides, I've got a busy weekend." She couldn't quite keep the pride out of her voice. "The bed and breakfast is full. Every room taken. That's the second weekend in a row that's happened."

"That's fantastic," I cried out. I couldn't be more pleased for her. She'd taken a huge risk, invested everything she had in turning the big, old house she'd inherited into a quality bed and breakfast. There were some challenges, of course, one of them being that Ballydehag wasn't a huge tourist center, the other being that my ancestor, Biddy O'Donnell, an evil old witch who'd been hanged for her crimes and refused to stay dead, had taken up residence in the home since she'd formerly had a property on that very site. Biddy was a big problem in my life. She was also family, which made it difficult to get rid of her.

Karen left, saying she'd see us both later at the pub.

When the door closed behind her, I turned to Kathleen. "What were you thinking, inviting Karen along?"

"If I didn't, she might have been suspicious. And I knew she'd never say yes. The only time Karen Tate gets her hands dirty is if she's cleaning up an old antique of hers. You won't find her in the garden digging in the muck. Don't worry, I know this village and most of the people in it. Even those who live outside of it. If they don't come into my shop to buy their food, I usually deliver it to them. There's not much in Ballydehag I don't know about, Quinn."

She said it almost like a warning.

Order your copy today! *A Poisonous Review* is Book 4 in the Vampire Book Club series.

A Note from Nancy

Dear Reader,

Thank you for reading *A Spelling Mistake*. I am delighted to write about an older, more experienced witch and very happy to find so many readers are enjoying older characters. I hope you'll consider leaving a review and please tell your friends who like paranormal women's fiction and cozy mysteries. Review on Amazon, Goodreads or BookBub.

If you enjoy paranormal cozy mysteries, you might also enjoy the *Vampire Knitting Club* - a story that NYT Bestselling Author Jenn McKinlay calls "a delightful paranormal cozy mystery perfectly set in a knitting shop in Oxford, England. With intrepid, late blooming amateur sleuth, Lucy Swift, and a cast of truly unforgettable characters, this mystery delivers all the goods."

Join my newsletter for a free prequel, *Tangles and Treasons*, the exciting tale of how the gorgeous Rafe Crosyer, from The Vampire Knitting Club series, was turned into a vampire.

I hope to see you in my private Facebook Group. It's a lot of fun. www.facebook.com/groups/NancyWarrenKnitwits

Until next time,
Happy Reading,

Nancy

ALSO BY NANCY WARREN

The best way to keep up with new releases, plus enjoy bonus content and prizes is to join Nancy's newsletter at NancyWarrenAuthor.com or join her in her private Facebook group www.facebook.com/groups/NancyWarrenKnitwits

The Great Witches Baking Show: Culinary Cozy Mystery

Gingerdead House - A Holiday Whodunnit

The Great Witches Baking Show Boxed Set: Books 1-3

Abigail Dixon: A 1920s Cozy Historical Mystery

In 1920s Paris everything is très chic, except murder.

Death of a Flapper - Book 1

Toni Diamond Mysteries

Toni is a successful saleswoman for Lady Bianca Cosmetics in this series of humorous cozy mysteries.

Frosted Shadow - Book 1

Ultimate Concealer - Book 2

Midnight Shimmer - Book 3

A Diamond Choker For Christmas - A Holiday Whodunnit

Toni Diamond Mysteries Boxed Set: Books 1-4

The Almost Wives Club

An enchanted wedding dress is a matchmaker in this series of romantic comedies where five runaway brides find out who the best men really are!

The Almost Wives Club: Kate - Book 1

Secondhand Bride - Book 2

Bridesmaid for Hire - Book 3

The Wedding Flight - Book 4

If the Dress Fits - Book 5

The Almost Wives Club Boxed Set: Books 1-5

Take a Chance series

Meet the Chance family, a cobbled together family of eleven kids who are all grown up and finding their ways in life and love.

Chance Encounter - Prequel

Kiss a Girl in the Rain - Book 1

Iris in Bloom - Book 2

Blueprint for a Kiss - Book 3

Every Rose - Book 4

Love to Go - Book 5

The Sheriff's Sweet Surrender - Book 6

The Daisy Game - Book 7

Take a Chance Boxed Set: Prequel and Books 1-3

For a complete list of books, check out Nancy's website at NancyWarrenAuthor.com

ABOUT THE AUTHOR

Nancy Warren is the USA Today Bestselling author of more than 100 novels. She's originally from Vancouver, Canada, though she tends to wander and has lived in England, Italy and California at various times. While living in Oxford she dreamed up The Vampire Knitting Club. Favorite moments include being the answer to a crossword puzzle clue in Canada's National Post newspaper, being featured on the front page of the New York Times when her book Speed Dating launched Harlequin's NASCAR series, and being nominated three times for Romance Writers of America's RITA award. She has an MA in Creative Writing from Bath Spa University. She's an avid hiker, loves chocolate and most of all, loves to hear from readers!

The best way to stay in touch is to sign up for Nancy's newsletter at NancyWarrenAuthor.com or join her private Facebook group facebook.com/groups/NancyWarrenKnitwits

To learn more about Nancy and her books
NancyWarrenAuthor.com

facebook.com/AuthorNancyWarren

twitter.com/nancywarren1

instagram.com/nancywarrenauthor

amazon.com/Nancy-Warren/e/B001H6NM5Q

goodreads.com/nancywarren

bookbub.com/authors/nancy-warren

Printed in Great Britain
by Amazon

28103324R00128